DO NOT ENTER! 1

FORBIDDEN PRESS! inc.
4824 Chemin Côte-des-Neiges
Suite 206
Montreal, Quebec H3V 1G4

Do not enter! 1 - For Boys Only. Caroline Heroux

Graphic Design: Anne Sol
Literary direction: Pierre Szalowski

ISBN: 978-2-925004-04-2

Legal Deposit: First trimester 2020 for Forbidden Press!
Les Éditions défendu! Inc/Forbidden Press! Do not Enter! 1 - For Boys Only.

Bibliothèque et Archives du Québec
Bibliothèque et Archives du Canada

CONTACT:
forbiddenpressbooks@gmail.com

DO NOT ENTER! 1

FOR BOYS ONLY

CAROLINE HÉROUX
IN COLLABORATION WITH CHARLES-OLIVIER LAROUCHE

OKAY. Where should I start?

Today is **August 5th** (sitting on my bed, in my room) and I am grounded **AGAIN**, because I nosed around {once again} in my ~~sister~~ half-sister Amelia's bedroom.

SO WHAT if I put a dead frog on her bed?

But **don't** tell my mom.

She screams her head off. (She's such a girl).

Amelia: Aaaaaaaaaaaargh!!! Mooo-ooom!!!

Too bad for her. She shouldn't be so **mean** to me all the time. Particularly in front of her friends.

Mom (mad): What were you thinking?
Me (shrugging): ...
Mom: Do you realize how scared your sister was?
Me: Please! It's not like she's never seen a frog before!?
Mom: Not a dead one in her bed!! Seriously, Charles, sometimes, I really wonder what goes on inside your head...

Me: It was just a joke! Haven't you EVER heard that word before? I tell you, there is NO sense of humor in this family!

Mom: It was a bad joke. And it was in bad taste. And as far as sense of humour goes, I am the first to laugh when something is funny.

She leaves my room without saying another word. Huh... Okay. What now? I guess I have to stay in here until dinner? **(She does that ALL the time).**

<u>But it was worth it:</u>

I can't stop smiling!!

**And it's a crazy big smile, which tells me it was really worth it!!!

P.S. ** I shouldn't have admitted to doing it, because mom couldn't **prove** I was to blame. **Unfair!** I should hire a lawyer. I have rights... right?

I should be allowed to defend myself properly. Better yet, I should complain to the commission of... uh... commission of...

WHAT EXACTLY?

THE C.K.W.W.C.A.T.B.S. (= commission of kids who want to complain about their big sister.).

TAKE THAT!

Seriously, my sister really gets on my nerves, with her long hair, make-up and too-short skirts. She thinks she's so cool... **BUT SHE IS so not!**

She and her boyfriend were kissing the other day...

 On the lips! (Gross)

When I lied and told her I filmed her, she screamed at me:

Melia: You're such an **IDIOT!**

And so, mom sent us both to our rooms (again), although it gave me time to think about my next "coup". Until, of course, my annoying little brother came in **10 minutes** later to... well, annoy me once again.

He doesn't leave me alone **EVER**, and he gets on my nerves **big time**. His name is **Arthur**. Oh, by the way, I'm

CHARLES

...BUT EVERYBODY CALLS ME:

CHARLIE

When he was younger, my little brother Arthur gave me that nickname.

It's *COOL* to have a nickname. I like it. Even if

CHARLIE is pretty common, and not my favorite.

*** Is it me or do I feel weird "talking" to a notebook? (I SAID NOTEBOOK, AND NOT DIARY).

> It feels good to say what I think. Also, it's not like I'm writing in a **real** diary.
>
> ** Only girls do that.

My older sister is AMELIA, but I call her GRANNY, because she's worse than a grandmother. I know it makes no sense, but she hates it, so... well, I like it. Everyone calls her MELIA.

DUH...

Not much difference. Arthur's nickname is Tutu. I swear, I AM NOT EVEN JOKING! Worst part? He doesn't mind it!!! **To be named after a ballerina's skirt!!** SERIOUSLY?! (not very manly).

I have a nickname for him, but it's not really nice, so I keep it to myself... you know, just in case my mom hears me. Which is more than possible because she hears and sees *ABSOLUTELY EVERYTHING!*

P.S. ** At first I thought every mother was the same, but my friends tell me no... Freaky.

My mom's incredible. She has eyes all over because she sees ABSOLUTELY everything!! Matched against her bionic ears, I have to be careful *WHAT I SAY!!* So I keep the nicknames to myself!

☺ By the way, Arthur has a twin sister, and her name is Lucy

What's her nickname?  Lulu!!

No kidding!!! TUTU & LULU!!!

Very simple. And very tacky. Lulu leaves me alone for the most part. But she trails behind Tutu like a sheep

BA-A-A!!

My little brother always bothers me when I'm with my friends and it annoys me.

Mom's voice: Charliiiiiiiiiiie!!!!!

UH-OH!

She's calling because we need to get our new uniforms.

School starts in **21 DAYS** (I'm not happy about it, but there's no choice).

Mom's voice: CHARLIE!

Have to go, she's getting impatient.

I doubt I'll write in this dia notebook again. I have **FAR MORE INTERESTING THINGS TO DO** than to waste my time in this... even if it soothes me to let it all out!

BYE BYE ~~DIARY~~ NOTEBOOK!!

Sniff

NOTEBOOK

Two days later...

AUGUST 7th

OKAY. So I am grounded in my room... again. Today is **August 8.** Instead of counting birds flying by my window, I might as well finish my story (not many birds... so time isn't really "flying by", ha ha). Where was I?

Oh, yes, my little brother. *OH NO, WAIT,* my big sister!

AMELIA.

or should I say **Granny.** She spends hours in front of the bathroom mirror, and it's always when I need to... well... go for... well, **NUMBER 2.** When that happens, I have to go to the first floor.
(where the whole family can hear me... uh... fart)

NIGHTMARE.

{ **THERE IS A FULL LENGTH MIRROR IN HER ROOM. CAN'T SHE STARE AT HERSELF THERE?** }

WHAT CAN SHE POSSIBLY BE LOOKING AT FOR SO MANY HOURS??? I don't get it. I would **NEVER** do that. I'd never waste so much time staring at myself.

I walk into her bedroom to get something.

Melia: What do you want?

OH, she's on FaceTime with her **BFF**

{=Best friends forever = annoying.}

Melia: You're interrupting!
Nana: Hey Charlie!
Me: Hi Nana! Haven't you seen my sister enough for one day?
Melia: Leave us alone!
Me: So, what's the latest gossip?
Melia: I said: Leave us alone!!
Me: Common, I'm curious. Who loves who nowadays?

Melia stands up to... hit me?

Melia: Hey, get out or I am calling mom!!
Me (faking to be afraid): Ooooooh, you scare me.

Honestly, I am really **SCARED**, but I can't show it. (Not of my sister, but of my mom and her magical powers.)

Me: Bye Nana.

He he

They are pathetic. **No life**. And when Melia's not on FaceTime with Nana, she is with **Simon**. Her boyfriend. At least, he is *TOTALLY COOL!!*

P.S. ****** I don't get why he loves my sister. I mean, she is nasty, and she gets those huge pimples on her face sometimes...

NIGHTMARE.™

So glad to be a man. well, a boy. *FUTURE MAN.* I'm only *11 YEARS OLD,* so I have to be careful, because I might also eventually get those huge, ugly, pimples. Just like a real

AUGUST 9th

In my room...

This time, I deserve it, because I broke Melia's nose.

NOT INTENTIONALLY

P.S. ******I (almost) swear.

I honestly never thought it would get this bad. I only wanted her to trip (**it happened this morning, in the kitchen**). It's not my fault if she landed on the fridge! Her nose was bleeding like hell. Just like a **HORROR MOVIE!**

BLOOD *EVERYWHERE*. My best friend, **Max**, steals his big brother's DVD's and we watch them together. We say we're playing Mario Bros on the Wii, but we watch **HORROR MOVIES!**

It's crazy!

My parents forbid me from watching these kinds of movies because they think I'll have **NIGHTMARES**.

UH, WHAT'S THE CONNECTION??

** I'm not a baby anymore.

OKAY. I admit, I don't like going downstairs by myself. <u>**NOT THAT I AM SCARED**</u>, but I strongly believe that it's smarter to go with a member of my family. Just in case... you know... there are **unwanted creatures** down there.

So, in regards to my sister, my dad had to take her to the hospital to get her nose fixed.

P.S. **I feel bad. I just wanted her to get hurt a bit.

THAT'S IT!

(I didn't wish for a broken nose... at least not that broken. I even tried to comfort her when she cried her heart out for an hour before leaving...)

The broken nose was a **BONUS**. I guess she got what she deserved for being mean to me sometimes.

No comment

August 11th

Sitting on my bed, in my room. It's *100%* unfair that I am being punished today. **TUTU** started the whole thing. Melia is still not speaking to me...

(I lay down, in order to notice, for the hundredth time, the bad paint strokes on the wall, next to where dad installed my **Darth Vader** ** poster. My room is *Star Wars* themed.)

** I don't feel like writing, but I have to let it out.

Why am I **ALWAYS** the grounded one!? I tried to protest, but mom grabbed me by the ear.

REALLY?!?

At my age??

Just like when I was 4! (My ear hurts.)

I am **so mad** I just want to destroy my room. It sucks, I can't play soccer with my friends. Summer's almost over, and it feels like I spent all of it in my room.

Come to think of it, I **CAN'T WAIT** for school to start! I'll have a break from my crazy

<u>One week later...</u>

August 17th

I just beat my own record!! I haven't been grounded in the last *7 DAYS!* (I sort of missed my ~~diar~~ **NOTEBOOK**... but only because I feel better when I say what I think.)

7 DAYS!!!

THAT'S HUGE!!!

Even my parents are worried about me. No way I am spending the few days left of summer inside.

NO WAY!!

August 19th

(**sitting on my bed, I realize my room needs a new paint job. Trying to calm down, but I want to kill someone... so to speak)

<u>Here's the story:</u>

I am having the time of my life playing soccer with my friends in front of my house.

TUTU shows up.

Tutu: What are you doing?
Me: Can't you see? We're playing soccer.
Tutu: Can I play too?
Me: No.
Tutu: Pleaaaaaaaase!!
Me: No.
Tutu: Yes.
Me: Hey, leave us alone!

But my brother grabs the ball and starts playing. I charge from behind and hit him **(just a little)** in the back.

Mom's voice: CHARLES!!!

Where the heck is she?!? I can't even see her?!

She charges from behind **(like I did to my brother)** and,

IN FRONT OF MY FRIENDS.

Mom: Did you just really do that?
Me: What? What did I do?
Mom: Hey, don't speak to me like that!

Parents have the right to do everything. Kids can never do *ANYTHING*. **Is she really going to ground me!?!** I didn't even do anything!! (**Almost**)

Mom: Wasn't breaking your sister's nose enough?
Me: What's the point?! I didn't even hit him hard!
Mom: In you room, NOW!

AAARGH!!!! I am raging. Boiling. I need to form my own country where kids will have rights!!

FOR EVERYONE!

All-you-can-eat Chocolate and soccer!!!!

No more school!!! Only RECESS!!!

Like any other great president, I must find a name first.

ANY IDEAS?

Fun!!

Freedom!!

...unlimited recess!!!!!!

shivers just walked in. That's my dog!

**Oops! I forgot to introduce him before!

I'm insulted!

Me: Hey, you! Come here, my big ball of hair!

We call him **shivers** as a joke, because he is **really** hairy, so he is **NEVER COLD!!** I love snuggling next to him on cold winter nights. He keeps me so warm!

He's worth a hundred **WOOL BLANKETS!!!** We have had him for almost three years, now.

I'm the best!

A friend of a friend of my dad's cousin had five puppies to sell, and dad decided to buy one. We had been begging our parents to get one for years.

But **Mom was right**, she's the one stuck taking care of him. *WHAT?* It's a nightmare to walk him, especially when it rains!

*Except when I really want something, then I offer to take over. (But never when it's too cold, raining... too hot, or when my favorite show is on TV.)

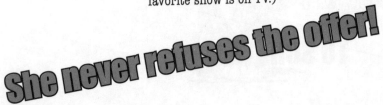

She never refuses the offer!

So, I'm in my room, and my stupid brother is whining for **NO REASON**.

P.S. ****NOTHING NEW**: He always cries for no reason at all.

And mom got mad at me in front of my friends.

A W K W A R D ! ! !

{ *AWKWARD* is my favorite expression. No one else says it. Oh, except the parrot in the movie *RIO!* }

Melia shows up right on time to see my mom grabbing my ear. Of course, she's laughing her head off!

In front of **my friends**. I'm going to make her pay. I was so ashamed. I'll get back at her when we start school. In front of **all of her friends**. I promise.

<u>Note to myself:</u> her nose is **off limits**...

Tomorrow will be **August 24th**.

BACK TO SCHOOL... yeah!

I'm chilling in my room, but I'm not on a *TIME-OUT* (for once). Although my mother wants me to hit the sack early tonight to be energized for my first shool day tomorrow. (**Might as well say I am on a time-out, because I **HATE** going to bed early. It's the worst thing in the world.)

I love it.

BORING. It's *8PM*. I'm *11*, almost *12*. (What? I just turned 11, but I'll be 12 eventually, **IN LESS THAN A YEAR!!**) I should be able to go to bed at *10 PM* **minimum**. My parents **(especially mom)** are such **DOWNERS**.

They are way too strict!

**At least she didn't force me to open a book. I hate reading. **

I do like to read, sometimes. Especially funny stories. I can go through a whole book in just a few hours if it's exciting.

I prefer writing to reading. Time goes by much faster. And they're **MY STORIES**, and not someone else's, so they are far more interesting!

I just... um... **YUCK!** Let's just say it doesn't smell so good in my room right now, I should open the window to **LET SOME FRESH AIR IN**. I had an omelet for dinner, that's probably what the smell of **ROTTEN EGGS** is from. My sister walks in at the same time.

Melia (smelling)**:** Oooh! Gross!
Me: What?
Melia: What's that smell?
Me: Oh? So your nose is "working again"?
Melia: You're a pig, Charlie.
Me: Leave, then! Next time, you should knock before entering! Haven't you noticed the sign on my door??

DO NOT ENTER!

Melia leaves me alone.

She never knocks, so I won't knock next time I go into her room -- to go through her things. *OOPS*, Mom's coming up the stairs!!

HURRY! BED TIME!!!

August 24th

BACK TO SCHOOL! I'm in Miss Howard's class.

Yeah!!! She's, like, the coolest teacher in the whole ~~world~~ school!! My old friend, Max, is in my class, as well as Jason and Tommy. There are a few girls, but they all ~~talk too much~~. They get on my nerves. I love being in my friends' class.

I look towards the door. *OOOOOOOOOOH!!!*

BOUM BOUM BOUM BOUM

Who's that girl who just walked in?? I've never seen her before. I **WOULD HAVE REMEMBERED!!**

Long brown hair, tall, deep green eyes, and that smile... ooooh... to die for, so to speak.

Is she new here?? Is she walking in my direction? Has she already noticed me??

She drops her bag and sits at the desk next to mine.

Her (holding out her hand): Hi, I'm Justine!
Me: Huh... (I grab her hand... It's very soft) Charles.
Justine: Hi Charlie. Nice to meet you.

Charlie. Hmm... quite 'INTIMATE' already. Not bad for a first encounter!

P.S. ** Oh, so she didn't choose "me". She had no choice but to sit next to me. All the other desks were taken.

P.P.S. ** I've never thought this before, but I hope we keep the same seats all year...

** Today was a half day and we went back home for lunch. Tomorrow, my mom's ham sandwiches will be back in my lunchbox again. Good, I loooove my mom's ham sandwiches! Frankly, that's all I eat. Seriously! Two slices of ham between two slices of bread. NOTHING ELSE. Sometimes, she uses a different bread. But the ham is always the same. My dad cooks it in the presto and it's awesome. (He adds brown sugar and beer on top of it.) AWESOME!!

OKAY, so what if I'm picky with my food? Mom is discouraged. She would like to make me something other than **ham sandwiches**. (**she's such a great cook!)

I promised her I'd make an effort this year and eat more often at the cafeteria, like my friends do. I don't want to be a *LOOOOOOOOSER* like **WILLIAM THOMPSON**. He's a huge looser. The biggest.

His glasses are so thick they look like bulletproof windows. HA HA HA! And if he keeps eating like a PIG like that, he's going to be like... uh, a big person. **He already is.

August 25th

In my room... barefoot... (I know that's not a very interesting detail, but I wanted to mention it anyway.) My mom is **OBSESSED: SHE THINKS WE MUST go to bed early in order to be rested. Only Melia **is allowed to go to bed later.** Makes sense, she's older than I am.

I'm the youngest.

She's **15**. We have the same dad, but her biological mom **died of cancer** a few days after giving birth to her. So Melia never really knew her. Worse, she blames herself for "KILLING" her mom. There is actually no relationship between **cancer** and giving birth. But my sister thinks that if her mom hadn't gotten pregnant, she wouldn't have had cancer. **I FIND IT SAD** that she blames herself. ~~It's really not her fault.~~

{ THANK GOD THAT DIDN'T HAPPEN TO MY MOM. }

My mom grounds me too often, but she's **STILL VERY ALIVE** and she tells me she loves me **EVERYDAY**. I moan every time, but I like to hear it.

P.S. ** My father works very hard, and we
don't see much of him during the week, but we
spend quality time with him on weekends. He owns
a dry cleaning company. That's why he works so hard.

We still haven't gotten homework yet **{I'm happy about that}**, but I have a feeling we'll be loaded next week. Okay, I'm tired. Going to bed, now.

It's *8:15PM*.

~~I might dream about Justine a bit before falling asleep.~~

I'm tired.

I hope he falls asleep quickly.

September 6th
(School. My classroom. English – Boring.)

Time flies faster when I'm at school. I exchanged notes with Max today during class. Our teacher is such a *LOOOOSER*. She wears army boots with a dress. **horrible boots with a horrible dress**. I'll bet she has a tattoo somewhere. She sure looks like someone who does. **I AM INTRIGUED**. How to find out? Anyway, she is way too old to *WEAR* those boots.

I MEAN, SHE MUST BE AT LEAST 30! **And she has an accent when she speaks English.** Josephine Leblanc. Not very English.

September 7th
(In class, 2nd row, near the window, 3rd seat)

Justine smiled at me today. And she laughed at my joke! **AT LEAST, I THINK SO.** Because someone else joked at the same time, so I am not *100% SURE IT WAS MY JOKE SHE WAS LAUGHING AT.*

    ** *50%* sure, I guess.
    *** But it's better than *0%*, right?

September 11th
(In class, same place: 2nd row, near the window, 3rd seat.)

Today, we talked about September 11, 2001 and what happened at the **World Trade Center**, in New York.

I went there once, but after 2001, so I didn't get to see the towers, but it was quite impressive to see the BIG HOLE THEY LEFT. **2000 people died that day**. Too many broken families, orphans, widows. What a tragedy.

Makes me sad just to think about it.

Miss Howard showed us pictures, and I watched videos on YouTube.

William Thompson SWEARS his father knew someone who knew someone (who knew someone?) who died jumping from TOWER #2. He rarely tells the truth, so I am not sure I believe him.

P.S. **But his father did live in New York, so it's not impossible. (unless he made up that his dad lived in New York? We never know with him. Aaargh... this is so confusing!)

FACT: My grandparents had dinner on top of one of the towers THREE DAYS BEFORE they went down. The restaurant was the one on top of TOWER #1 (or #2?). It was called... UH, I don't remember the name, but my grandma told me it was EXCELLENT. I think there was the word WORLD in it?

She says someone should invent SMALL SINGLE PARACHUTES for people working in towers higher than 10 stories. They could jump out of a building without killing themselves. Ooooh, I can't think about it without shivering. I'd rather die than jump. Let's just say I am not really the "jumper" type.

Me neither.

A FEW MINUTES LATER, after reflecting on it. No. I'd rather jump than die.

Come to think of it, you can die jumping from the roof of a house, right? Does that mean every house should get the parachutes?

*** HMM... if I sold them worldwide, I'd become the youngest, richest guy in the world. Maybe then, Justine would find me cool (and attractive??)?

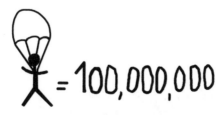

= 100,000,000

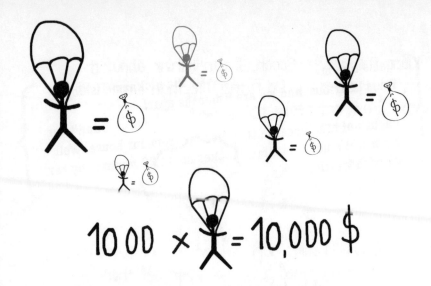

$$1000 \times \text{人} = 10{,}000 \ \$$$

My mom says **everybody** remembers what they were doing on *SEPTEMBER 11, 2001*. It was an historic event, and it left its mark on **everybody** forever. The whole world changed that day, my dad says. Anyway, we sure learned what **Al-Qaïda** was and who **Ben Laden** was.

What I also learned is that we must take our shoes off when we go through security at the airport. And forget about joking about anything, because customs and security officers have **no sense of humor**.

I guess they can't take any situation lightly. Just in case...

✳✳✳

Tommy's coming to my house on *SATURDAY*. *COOOOL!!!* We'll have soooo much fun! Of all my best friends, he's like my **BEST** best friend.

I also like my COUSIN JOEY-ANTHONY. His nickname is Joje. He is hilarious, and we are 8 months apart (but he is a giant! So much taller than me! I look like a dwarf next to him!) I don't see enough of him, because they live far from our house. Well, for me, it's not THAT far, it takes about 20 minutes by car. 45 with traffic.

It's about 27 miles north of where we live, and mom jokes that you need a **passport** to get there! *HAHA!!*

September 12th

(In my room, sitting at **my desk**... I know... that's unusual.)

Things to do with Tommy on Saturday:

* Play hockey.
* Gossip about our older sisters —
secretly, in my room. Tommy is also stuck with one, but she's a few months younger than Melia. She's fourteen, and her name is **Geoli** (pronounced "jo-lie" – like "pretty" in French- but she's really not).
Weird name, but I don't ask questions.

* Talk about people in our class (including William Thompson).
* Play on the Wii {coooool}.
* Eat mac & cheese and Rice Krispies squares. (or mom's awesome brownies— YEAH!!)

That Saturday...

I don't care about the date

** WORST DAY OF MY LIFE...

Tommy's **no longer** my friend. He got here at ten this morning, and and asked to watch..... Harry Potter and the Sorcerer's Stone. **(HIS FAVOURITE).**

**No problem so far...

So, we watched the movie together. But, after lunch **(with my two leeches, Tutu et Lulu)**, here's what happened:

Tommy: Let's watch Harry Potter again!
Me: What? No way!

Tommy: What do you mean, no way? I am your guest.

Me: Tommy, we should play outside instead, or play a board game. But I don't want to watch a movie again.

Tommy: Well, in that case, I am going home!

HE RUINED THE WHOLE DAY.

Also, when we were watching the movie, Tutu came to ask me a question, and Tommy started yelling at him for interrupting. (He didn't actually yell, **but close enough)**.

(**He was watching the movie for the 23rd time! I mean, seriously?!?)

I know my brother can be a pain sometimes, but there's no reason for acting this way.

Tommy's the worst.

I should have asked my friend Max to come instead. I am sure I would have had more fun.

<u>Worse part of my day (if that's even possible):</u>
My mom asked me to help Tutu with his
Star Wars Lego while she prepared dinner...
Worst day of my life. ☹☹☹☹☹☹☹

** {Oh! Chocolate pancakes for desert?
YUM! Not a bad day, after all!} ☺☺

I know how to get a smile on Charlie's face. He he.

October 3rd

Walking out of Costco with dad. We bought tons of
candy for ~~Halloween~~ ~~Halloowe'en~~

HALLOWE'EN!!!**

** I know, I know, we're a bit early: But my
dad is always worried about being short on
candy.

My dad's the coolest (especially when mom's not around).
Today is the twins' **birthday**, and Lulu's overexcited. .

We're eating at my favorite italian restaurant. They make the best pizza in the WORLD!! Dad and I went to get another **Star Wars Lego** for Tutu (yep, another one!), and Lulu's getting a new doll mom ordered a few weeks ago.

(IT WAS DELIVERED LAST WEEK, BUT SHHH! IT'S A SECRET!!)

Mom needs to make birthday cakes for each of the twins, so she doesn't have time to run errands today. I (gladly) volunteered to go with dad and help him out. **That way, I won't have to babysit the twins.** Melia has that dirty job while mom bakes!

P.S. **Her boyfriend Simon is home. They broke up last week, but got back together this week. HUGE MISTAKE.

{For him, anyway}

We're celebrating the twins' birthday tomorrow at an interior fun park with lots of different slides and games... and ~~lots~~ too many

EIGHT-YEAR-OLDS.

- **NIGHTMARE!!**
- **BOMB.**
- **BORING.**
- **MAJOR BORE.**
- **UG, WORST THING IN THE WORLD.**

Me: I don't want to go. I don't mind staying home alone.

> **Ya right. I'll try to stay busy, and try not to think about the "un-invited" guests that could break and enter and kill me.

Mom: You're coming, and it's non negotiable!
Me: But moooooooooooom!!
Mom: I said NO! And I don't want to hear another word about it. Understood?

Geez. Calm down. It was just a thought. No need to get all excited and mad. But, of course, I obey without moaning.

I ABSOLUTELY HATE kids' birthday parties. They suck. They all scream and run all over the place, I get dizzy. I should invent a time machine and transport myself to the future so that I miss the party. Wouldn't that be nice?

> *P.S.* ****Note to self:** I must find a way to invent a time machine. We'll do it when I form my new country. Oh! We should also be able to go back in time, you know, that could be fun sometimes. Also, while we're at it, I have to remind myself to invent those small parachutes. I'm going to be so rich!

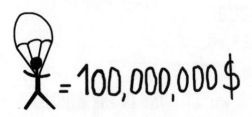 = 100,000,000 $

** I'll send grandma royalties. After all, it was her idea originally.

How about dog parachutes?

October 4th

The twins' party was *SICK!* Lulu has a new friend named **Charlotte**. And guess who her older sister is?!?

JUSTINE!!!

The ~~cute~~ girl in my class! She drove her sister to the party (with her mom, of course, because Justine doesn't drive) and we SPOKE !!!
TOOOOO COOL!!!

Here's how it went:

Me: Hi.

Justine: Hi.

Me (aiming at Charlotte): Is that your sister?

J.: Yes.

Me: I didn't know you had a sister.

J.: ...

Me: You drove here with her?

(Duh, obvious, no??)

J.: Yes.

Me: Coooool.

Oh Gosh. That didn't go very well.

<u>In the car, on the way home after the party:</u>
Er... Justine probably thinks I'm an idiot. I acted like a moron in front of her. I think. Maybe?

<u>Later, end of pm – in the kitchen, nibbling on chips...</u>

** Come to think of it, I *KNOW* Justine thinks I'm an idiot. I acted like one. *DARN IT!*

During the evening:
(In my room, sitting on the floor, in the corner, between my desk and the only electrical outlet in my room ...)

I can't stop thinking about Justine and what happened today. I suck **BIG TIME**.

****AAAARGH!** I hope she doesn't spread the word about what I said to her friends. I looked like a fool... I could have responded more intelligently. I am (intelligent), after all... Sometimes anyway. She must think I am such a loser... even if she laughed at my joke in class, the other day. the **whole class** laughed, so it doesn't really count.

In the middle of the night... I wake up with a start:

** *DAAAAAAARN* IT!!!

For sure she thinks I'm a *MAJOR LOOOOOSER*. I gotta find something nice to do at school to impress her.

• Become president of the class – almost impossible, it's always Jonathan.
• Get *100%* in my next essay – impossible to get *100%* in writing. Even for Minh-Khai, the **BRAIN** of the class.
• Be the funniest. Impossible... I think. Even if I'm much funnier than Jonathan and Nathan.

October 5ᵗʰ

OKAY.

Not only am I grounded in my room **(not saying why because it's a bit embarrassing)**, but I can confirm Justine thinks I'm a *TOTAL LOOOOSER*.

She didn't look at me today, **and** she didn't answer me when I said: **HI!**. (I didn't say it loud = not sure she heard me.) My ~~stup~~ sister... Why did she have to be friends with **Justine's sister**? Might as well admit to myself that my **LIFE IS RUINED**. I have twin **"life ruiners"** for siblings. I know that's not an expression, but this is **my** notebook, and I can write *WHATEVER I WANT* in it!! It's the only place where I can say what I want without being reprimanded.

I feel you, Charlie.

And Tommy is still mad at me for the other day. *REALLY??* I am sooooo glad I have Max. He is much **nicer**. And we get along so much better. *MUCH BETTER*. Who needs Tommy and **Harry Potter** after all? Don't get me wrong,

I loooove **HARRY POTTER** (my fave is #7, part 2) but twice in the same day? **SAME MOVIE** twice in one day is a bit much, *NO???*

> ** especially when the weather outside is awesome!!

October 7th

(In the kitchen, I hand mom a sheet from the teacher that I didn't bother reading because, frankly, I don't care.)

** NOOOOOOOOOO!?!
SHE STARES AT ME.

Mom: Please don't tell me??
Me: What?
Mom: The letter?
Me: What does it say?

Her face drops.

Mom: You didn't read it?

Er... Not really... no.
She hands it to me. Now, I'm a bit curious to know what it says, but I still don't feel like reading it.

Me: I just gave it to you!
Mom: Read it, you'll undestand. **(She shouts)** Twins!! Get here, right away, please!

They get down faster than **THE FLASH**. Amazing how they do it. I think they were listening from the other side of the door.

Mom: I need to check your hair. There's an outbreak of lice at school.
Me: WHAT? Are you kidding?
Lulu: How do you know?
Mom: Charlie just brought a letter from school.
Tutu: How come he didn't know?
Me: I knew!
Tutu: No, you didn't, you just said "WHAT?".
Me: Aaaargh Shut up!
Mom: Charles!??
Me: Sorry. (To Tutu) Just show your head and stop asking stupid questions.
Mom: Be nice, Charles.
Me: Sorry!

    ** Did I sort of forget she was there?

Mom (checking Lulu's hair): DAMN! (she shouts - again) Honeyyyyy!?! Can you rush to the pharmacy and get lice treatment shampooooo??? The twins have lice!!
Me: WHAT?
Tutu: Stop saying "what?". It's really annoying.

Me: Hey, stop it! You have lice. This is all YOUR fault!

Personally, I think mom **IS MAKING IT UP**, I mean, she always panics **for no reason**. Because she read the letter, she's imagining seeing lice on the twins' heads. She just wants all of us to do a treatment... for **PREVENTION**. I know her. But I can argue all I want, it's not going to work. I'll have to get **LICE SHAMPOO** in my hair, too.

I knew it. She wants all of us to do the treatment **JUST IN CASE**. And of course, there is a rush. We must do it **NOW**.

An hour later...

The whole family is sitting in the kitchen, shower caps on our heads for *THE NEXT 15 MINUTES*, looking like fools.

It's only been *TWO MINUTES AND FORTY-TWO*,

FORTY-THREE, FORTY-FOUR... seconds (!!) and I feel like my skull's about to peel off. NIGHTMARE.

I hate doing this, and it's the THIRD TIME in SEVEN YEARS. I'd rather die. (so to speak). And I shouldn't even be doing it! Mom didn't find anything in my hair, but she still insists I do it JUST IN CASE. She drives me crazy. Always panicking for no good reason.

I would really like a treatment, please.

We'll have to do another one in two DAYS.

Not only that, but she's washing all the sheets in the house, stuffed animals, cushions! EVERYTHING is getting "BURNED" in the washing machine's hot water cycle.

If she could fit the sofas in there, she would. Crazy.

I can, however, confirm that a shower cap doesn't look good on Melia. I took a picture of her without her knowing... as a back up for a future blackmail scheme. HA HA.

If a single LOUSE survives this "operation", it deserves the title of WORLD CHAMPION. The James Bond of lice. Mom went through every single corner of the house...

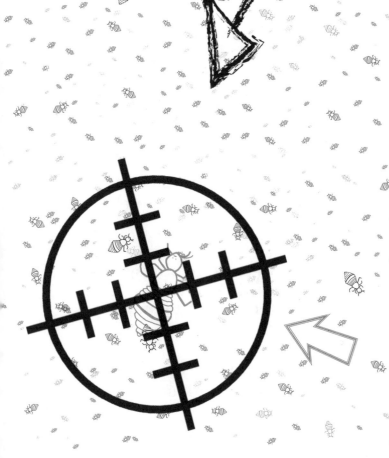

I did say please...

October 8th

(Cafeteria at school. Me = sitting at the second table left of the window, uh, I mean right... uh, it depends from where you're looking...)

Kevin (another 6th grader) knocked over William Thompson's plate at lunch. Of course, he did it on purpose, and William had spaghetti all over him. When the supervisor asked whose fault it was, William lied and said he tripped. He always lies about stuff like that, otherwise he knows he's going to get it from Kevin...

> ... and his three stooges. They're all stupid. **I nicknamed them idiot #1, idiot #2, idiot #3.

Maybe I shouldn't laugh, but it was hilarious to see it. Kevin and his stooges always pick on William.

I know it's wrong to laugh, but it was just a joke. It's not like they hurt him, right?

William's not laughing at all. **(no sense of humour?)**
Girls don't find it funny either, but who cares? They're
all **feather brains**.

JUSTINE INCLUDED.

Except when she laughs at my jokes. We don't talk
much. Well, not enough, in my opinion. I must find a
way to get the conversation going... but how?

> • Cracking more and better jokes.
> • Leaving my tests with good
> grades (when applicable) on my desk,
> so she can see them.
> • Uh... tbd (= to be determined)...

October 10th

(In class, sitting at my desk.)

It's **OFFICIAL**. I am a *TOTAL LOOOOOSER*.
This is why...

Ms. Howard: ... and the man answered: No, I was just sipping my coffee!
The whole class (including me): HA! HA! HA! HA!

PRRRRRRT!!!

OMG! Did that sound just come out of my body?
It wasn't the biggest fart, but it resonated, and I am sure Justine heard it.

She looks at me and smiles. **I WANT TO DIE.**

If she thought I was a loser before, she must think I am a *MEGA LOOOOOOOSER NOW*. Unless I get those parachutes going and sell them and get very rich, very quickly. I am never setting foot in school *EVER AGAIN!* I guess I feel how William Thompson might feel sometimes.

Not that I think about him.

IDEA: I should be "sick" tomorrow. And Friday's a ped day. ON MONDAY, it'll be FOUR DAYS off of school. Maybe Justine will have forgotten about the ~~fart~~ sound?

Good luck with that.

Later - that evening...
(Hiding under the blankets, in bed, so that no one finds me.)

** Thank God it didn't smell... NOT THAT IT MAKES A DIFFERENCE.

She heard and I'm done.

October 11th
(in bed, under my sheets.)

Mom didn't believe me this morning when I told her I didn't feel well and shouldn't go to school. Doesn't she get that I'd rather die than be made a fool of?

Mom (taking the thermometer out of my mouth): I knew it! No temperature.
Me: But mooom! I really don't feel well!
(Cough! Cough!)
Tutu: He's faking!
Me (mad): Mind your own business!!
Mom: Tutu go downstairs. (To me) Stop this nonsense and get dressed quickly! We're running late.

She stands up and leaves the room... I want to die. This is so embarrassing. I never want to see Justine again. I know she heard me...

October 14th
(Near the fence of the school's courtyard.)

Kevin and Justine were in a deep conversation after lunch. She kept laughing and flinging her hair like a... a... girl.

"Oh! Kevin! you are soooo funny!"

PFF... She's no better than the others.

October 26th

(Relaxing in my bed and it feels great. Shivers is lying next to me. He's so comfy.)

It was raining this morning when I woke up. But it's so cold outside, it's unbearable.

No way I am trick or treating in the costume I chose. I am supposed to be a surfer. And a surfer is always dressed in **SHORTS AND A T-SHIRT**.

I should be a snowboarder instead. I'll be much warmer. And snowboarders are super cool. **THEY'RE LIKE SURFERS, BUT ON SNOW, RIGHT?**

October 31st

In front of the house (<u>Traditional picture:</u> my siblings and me, standing in front of our house like idiots, wearing our Halloween costumes.)

So, it's not that cold after all tonight, but I am very happy with my **HARRY POTTER COSTUME** (competing with Tommy, haha!). It's not so original (**I saw three other Harrys on my street alone**), but I am warm. **MOST IMPORTANT.**

I know! I should have been **Chewbacca**

(= the beast from *Star Wars*). Then I would have been really hot!!

MOM DRESSED UP AS A... (YUP) WITCH.

<u>No comment...</u>

He he.

My cousin Joje dressed as a **cheeseburger**. And his little bro, Laurent, was a **hot-dog**. Of course he was, because he could eat sausages three meals a day!! Whenever he has dinner at our house and dad cooks sausage, he eats at least three!

I collected a huge bag full of candy. I'm so cooooool when it comes to Halloween. The coolest. I always get the most candy.

The twins didn't get that much. It's as if they didn't care. They kept whining the whole time, and they almost drove me *MAD*.

It's impossible to do something fun without them crying, whining, or complaining. It SUCKS, BIGTIME. I just can't stand them sometimes.

I love them.

I'm going to hide my candy in my room because mom always puts it in a closet somewhere, and then it disappears after a few days... I don't get it. WEIRD. My dad loves to eat candy in front of the TV at night, and it drives my mom nuts.

Weird fact: When I went to dad's office the other day, I noticed a bowl of Halloween candies. They looked a lot like MINE. When I asked his secretary where they came from, she told me he's the one who brought them... coincidence??

***

By the way, Justine dressed up as a cat, but I didn't see her. Max did, and he told me. I'll bet she looked good.

I love Halloween!

November 6th

(Sitting on my bed. I am grounded because I dipped Melia's toothbrush in lemon juice. *BIG DEAL*. I tell you, there is no sense of humour in this family).

It **SNOWED/RAINED** all day and it's FREEZING. Impossible to play outside, and the humidity is going through our bones.

I teased Melia at lunch today in front of her friends. Of course, she told mom, and **I am grounded** tonight. Unbelievable! Her word against mine, and mom believes **her?**

No comment.

OOH... I can't wait to become Prime Minister of my own country. I have to find a name:

- Zombieland?
- Planet Cool?
- Charlieland?

P.S. ** I should ask my cousin Joje, he always has the best ideas. It seems as if all the names are already used, doesn't it??

Unfair! It's like mom feels sorry for Melia, just because she doesn't have a mom anymore. But I can't say it or I'll get in trouble. Come to think of it, that's not really a nice thing to say.

(I wouldn't want to be in her shoes)

<u>I did win on one thing</u>: I can go to bed at *8:30PM* (but I can "stretch" it to *8:45PM* by protesting and whining that I am not tired.).

ONE STEP AT A TIME.

Max can go to bed at *9PM* every night. Lucky him (his mom is not as strict as mine, but, then again, none of my friend's moms are as strict as mine...). I noticed that Kevin and Justine talk a lot at school. Must be because he's older...

** He failed 4th grade and had to do it again. Not cool. I'd say he's a loser... but I would never say it out loud. He's kind of scary.

Aside from the fact that doing 4ᵀᴴ *GRADE* a second time is for looosers... What's the big deal about older guys? Anyway, I don't really care if Justine doesn't talk to me as much. Girls are such idiots anyway.

*I'm sure I'd have a lot to discuss with her, though.

November 9th

**(School playground, just in front of the metal trash can – the one hanging from the fence, where students stick their chewing gum...)

Kevin threw an **ICE BALL** in William's face today. It wasn't funny, but it was kind of funny. William **had a nose bleed** and had to go to the infirmary.

I was laughing (a little), but Justine wasn't at all. It was bleeding quite a bit. Down on his SCARF. William is going to get in trouble at home because the scarf is made of cashmere or something expensive.

WHO CARES? Once again, the guard didn't see anything. She is blinder than the blind, I tell you, blind to the bones, if that's even possible. She never sees anything.

** ☺ William cried like a baby.

P.S. ** Joje tells me that they also have a blind guard at his school. She's close to *90 YEARS-OLD OR SOMETHING...* OK, she's not that old, but very close.

** She should wear better glasses. (talking about our guard, not Joje's).

November 30th

Chilling in my bed – Tutu comes in to bother me, so I get up. *&?%$$#@# ☹☹

Tutu: Wake up Charlie! We're going skiing today!

Melia complains again, as usual. She wants to stay here with Simon, but dad insists on her coming with us. She could use the time outdoors. I agree. She's quite pale... Hey, as far as I am concerned, she should go out more

often, and for longer *PERIODS OF TIME*. The house would be much quieter.

I found her diary in her room and read a few pages:

« If she thinks I'm going to forgive her this time, she's wrong... » blah blah blah... I'm sooooo not buying her a birthday present, hopefully she'll get that I'm mad at her. » blah blah blah.

What a complete waste of time! Unbelievable the time wasted on writing such stupid things! At least the stories I write are interesting. Nothing to do with what girls write. It's not a diary but a notebook anyway... right?

<u>Oh, here's something interesting:</u>

« Nick complimented me on my dress today.
I wonder what it means. I think he "likes" me. OMG!
He's soooo cute. A lot more than Simon.
But I can't really say it, especially not to Nana...
She would never forgive me. »

I should tell Simon. Nick is his best friend. Wouldn't I be doing a good deed, from one guy to another? It's unfair that Simon doesn't know. I should tell him. Between men, we have to stick together if we want to survive as the... the... um... male species...

So there/Right?.

P.S. ** I'm excited to go skiing with my cousins. Especially Joje, because he likes to go in the woods, even if our parents don't want us to go there. They say it's too dangerous... (rolling my eyes...)

December 6th
In my room, sitting at my desk. I am a bit shaken up about what Miss Howard told us today.

There are so many mass shootings around the world that they almost can't keep track anymore. It really gives me the chills to hear about it.

There are too many people with mental illness, or with issues on this planet, and it's worse in countries where you are allowed to legally buy and carry guns. Anyone can just have a bad day and shoot someone else just because they feel frustrated about something.

BOOM! Watch out people, I am having a bad day and you're going to pay for it. It's unacceptable, yet it goes on every day...

When I get older, I will try to stop or prevent violence from happening, especially to innocent people. I will do that on top of my real work, during my spare time.

P.S. ** In my future country, there will be laws against guns and violence. But first, I must find a name for my country:

- Peace country
(ouch... It's a little too message from God)
- Violence-free country
(could I find a worse name??)
- Drop your weapons!
(I should go to bed, my head's really not into it tonight...)

Good idea!

December 10th

**(Near the school, it's raining outside... No more doubts about global warming.)

Melia mocked me today. I was playing with my friends and she walked passed me with her friends Simon, Nana, and Nick.

Melia: Hey jerk.
Me: Hey, big a***.
Melia: Still devastated because Justine is not talking to you? **(to her friends)** He cries all the time in his room.

ME = 0
MELIA = 10

TO MYSELF: How does she know THAT???

(OUCH!!!) All my friends are staring at me like I'm a dork. **I must react quickly.**

Me: No, I cry laughing at all the stories I read in your diary! I know them by heart now. **(To Nick)** She thinks you're way cuter than Simon.

**ME = 10
MELIA = 0**

OOOH!! You should see Melia's jaw dropping to the floor.

     ** And Simon's...
     ** And Nick's...
     ** And all her friends'...

She's so shocked she can't bend down to pick her jaw up from the floor and put it back... Huge tension between Simon and Nick... and **MELIA**.

That's when I found out that **Nana**, Melia's BFF, was **dating Nick**. Didn't know that before. I wish I'd been there when the two of them "talked about it" in private...

P.S. ** I'll read it in her diary in a few days anyway... Ha ha.
**Mom is soooo mad I'm being grounded for the whole week.

(We're in the kitchen.)
Mom: How did you find that out?
Me: Er... I sort of read it somewhere...
Mom: <u>In her diary</u>! Do you know what a DIARY is??
Me: ...
Mom: Answer me!!!!
Me: Yeah, sort of...
Mom: Not only do you have no right to go through your sister's private stuff, but I don't want you in her room without permission!

Me: Wait a minute! She goes into my room without permission!

Mom: I'll talk to her.

Me: You should also punish her!

Mom: Don't speak to me in that tone! Go think in your room now, and don't come down before dinner, got it?

Me: Okay...

I feel like a *TOTAL LOOSER* (**but not really guilty!). And I know Melia was listening, and so were the twins... Well, I'm pretty sure, anyway.

** My little brother inherited my mom's superpowers:

- he hears everything;
- he sees everything;
- he's everywhere;
- it's really freaky.

Runs in the family. He he.

My sweet Lulu brought me her wubby blanket to cheer me up. She's so sweet, she always brings me things when I'm grounded.

P.S. **What I like the most is when she brings me food because, besides writing in the book, I can't do much. I already know by heart every little fault in the paint job on my room's walls.

L O O S E R

December 11th

(At the end of the hall leading to the gym, there's a black plastic garbage can. **This is an important detail in my story.**)

I might be a **fool and an idiot** for some people (ref.: Melia), but there are things in life I can't accept or agree to. <u>**EXAMPLE:**</u> Nastiness. Like teenagers being mean to older people, or just people in general.

HERE'S THE STORY...

Today, *KEVIN* + *IDIOT #1* + *IDIOT #2* + *IDIOT #3* made a fool of William, as usual. So far, no problem. (We are sort of used to it.)

They **always** ridicule him in front of the whole school. Everybody laughs (even me...), even when it's not so nice. But today, fat boy (we call him that sometimes) needed his pump. {he is ~~hastm astmatiq~~ asthmatic} and Kevin took it away from him. That's less funny.

Tutu is also asthmatic, and when he needs his pump, **HE NEEDS IT BIG TIME!** So I followed Kevin and his gang (without being seen) and got the pump back from the trash can Kevin threw it in. (the one at the end of the hall = see the one I mentioned earlier with December 11, that one.).

I ran to catch up with William who was going to the infirmary and I gave him his pump. He took a few **PUFFS** right away and I could tell he felt better almost on the spot. When he finally felt better, a *FEW SECONDS LATER*, he said to me:

William: Thanks Charlie.
Me: You're welcome. (long pause) Kevin's an idiot.
William: Really? Then why do you always laugh when he intimidates me?

(Er, mega discomfort on my part.)

Me: Er ...
William: Thanks anyway for what you did. I really appreciate it.

As I am watching William walk away, I promise myself I will never laugh again. Just because it's not funny.

NOT FOR HIM, AND NOT FOR ANYONE.

THIS **HAS** TO STOP.

William is right. This is called **BULLYING**. Miss Howard has mentioned it in class a few times (I think ** er... but I don't always listen 100% TO WHAT SHE SAYS).
We must

DENOUNCE IT

instead of **encouraging it**. Not only because it could end badly, but because it's just wrong!

But I'm allowed to bully Melia... she's my sister, so rules don't apply the same way, right? I just have to make sure mom doesn't find out...

P.S. ** My cousin Joje tells me there is also bullying at his school, but he's good because he's such a giant that no one dares to make fun of him! My cousin is nice to everyone, and he likes to "protect" some of the kids.

THERE'S A second scene TO MY STORY.

* *(Still in the hallway, near the trash can, because I haven't moved yet.)

Something interesting happened... It's actually VERY interesting.

When I turned around to go back outside (right after giving William his medication), guess who was standing there??

JUSTINE!!
She saw everything and heard everything.

Me: ...
She: (Big smile on her face)
Me: ...

{ My face is red as a fire truck. I am so shy I'm looking down and notice a crack on the floor
** I'm staring at it because I am sooooo shy. }

She (moving towards me): That was nice of you...
Me: (I shrug) ...
She: You're not an idiot like Kevin ...
Me: ...

I can hear myself swallowing.

(She leans forward and **kisses me on the cheek**)

Me: (red like two tomatoes)
She: ... (she gives me a last look before going)
Me: ....

OH YESSSSSSS!!!!!

I know that November 11 is Remembrance Day, but for me, *DECEMBER 11* is the one I'll remember all my life. I will definitely sleep well tonight, even if I'm grounded for slapping Tutu. **HE DESERVED IT.**
(But it doesn't matter today because I feel good.)

December 20th

(In my room, on my bed. My door is closed. I can't lock it, unfortunately, because if I could...)

**I am grounded because mom found me snooping around Melia's room (but AFTER I had time to read a few pages of her diary, ha ha).

I know, I know, I shouldn't have. But it's so tempting! Haven't had much time to read anything in the past few weeks because I had to study. Justine and I have spoken a bit more, and we smile at each other once in a while in class.

Kevin's a looooooser... 😊 "Loooser" with a...

CAPITAL « L » ON THE FOREHEAD.

"L" for Love!!!

December 22nd

(At the cafeteria = it's a bit hectic because everybody's excited that we'll be off for the holidays in a few hours.)

We exchange **gifts in class**. Miss Howard prepared loot bags for everyone. *COOL*. Max's mom baked **cupcakes** for the whole class, and mine made **CHOCOLATE CHIP COOKIES**. She can be cool, sometimes.

> ***Er**, only when she doesn't punish me, of course.

JUSTINE came up to talk with me at recess...

Justine: Hi.
Me: Hi.
Justine: What are you doing during the Holidays?
Me: I'm going to my grandparents' in Florida.
Justine: Cool.
Me: You?

I'm a bit more comfortable when I speak to her now and I can almost look **HALF INTELLIGENT** in front of her.

Justine: We're going to cel--...

I feel a hand on my shoulder before she gets to finish her sentence. **I turn around**. Kevin is standing tall, his three stooges behind him. He crosses his arms and so do the three clowns. He makes the same face he does

when he's about to lose it with William... *UH OH.*
I ~~smail~~ ~~smo~~ smell trouble.

Kevin: What do you want from her?
Me: Er...
Kevin: You think you're so cool and you take the liberty of pissing on my territory?
Me: Er...

> *P.S.* ** Boy, I wish my cousin Joje were here right now to defend me. He could beat him up... um, I mean, scare him or strongly suggest he leave me alone. And Kevin would, because my cousin is the scariest, when he wants to be.

Justine: Leave him alone!
Kevin: Mind your own business.
Me: ... **I can't speak. I sure look:

- stupid
- moronic
- like an idiot
- like an imbecile
- like a jerk
- moronic
- hum, I think I just said that... but I don't care.

Kevin: Cat got your tongue?
Me: Er...

I try to shake my head: *NO,* but my body can't seem to be able to move (= terror-stricken), I already feel Kevin's fist on my left cheek, er, I mean, right, because he's right-handed... hm, come to think of it, because Kevin is right-handed, his fist will land on my *LEFT CHEEK.* Either way, it'll hurt like crazy.

Kevin: Aw ... you're such a moron.

He raises his hand and I step back with fear. Okay, now I truly understand the meaning of bullying and it's **NOT COOL**.
** Even more so in front of Justine.

Me: ...
Kevin: You're such a whimp!
Me: ...

P.S. ** Nothing's coming out of my mouth. I don't understand why, I'm usually so good at having come backs for Melia when we argue. But now, **NOTHING-NESS, TOTAL BLANK**. Kevin's right, I am a moron.

Kevin: Whass'up? Your mommy's not here to change your diaper?

His buddies are laughing. I want to tell him to leave my mother out of it, but I doubt it's the right time.

Me: ...

I just can't believe nothing is coming out of my mouth. I can't help it but I am really freaked out right now. He should really make it quick because, honestly, a few more minutes and I'll pee in my pants, and then it'll be really embarrassing.... Worse than farting in class.

NOTE TO SELF: **Shouldn't Justine intervene??
I mean, aren't ALL girls sassy and insolent? Why isn't
she saying anything?

Kevin: Hey?? I'm talkin' to you!?!
Me: Leave me alone! You jerk.

P.S. ** I finally spoke, but when I see
Kevin's face, I regret it right away.

OH OH. I see anger in his eyes, and he raises
his hand to hit me. I close my eyes, hoping it'll be less
painful when his hand HITS MY CHEEK. I hear

(but felt nothing?!?)

I OPEN MY EYES.

Kevin is knocked out, on the floor.

Me: ????? (Total confusion. What just happened?)

I SEE WILLIAM!!!

He's standing in front of Kevin, his fist still in the air.

Me: ...

My legs are so shaky I can barely stand.

Kevin: ☹☹☹☹
Justine: ...
Everybody: ...
Me: ....
William (To Kevin): You bully him one more time and you will need dentures. Understood?
Kevin: **

** He tries to put his jaw back in its place. His lip is bleeding, but his ego is even worse off. THE WHOLE school witnessed what just happened... well, at least half of it.

** Okay, Okay. Maybe not half of the students, but there's a lot of people. I swear... I would say about 20.

William (Red with anger): Hey, moron!! I'm talking to you!
(To myself — cool, he's repeating the same words Kevin just used on me.)
Kevin: ... (= he nods his head YES)
Everybody: ...
William: Glad we understand each other.

William's **fist** is still ready to hit again...

William (to me): You alright?
Me: ...

I *NOD*. I have to say, my jaw is hurting for Kevin's. That was a huge knock. Not that I disagree with what William just did! It was well deserved.

Mrs. Diane, our **blind** supervisor, **suddenly not so blind**, walks up to us:

Mrs. D: What's going on here?
Kevin (pointing at William): He hit me!! (He is almost crying) I didn't do anything and he punched me!!
Mrs. D: Is that true, William?

> *P.S.* ****** No. But yes. Kevin did nothing **TODAY,** but it was long overdue.

Because William defended me, it's my turn to return the favour...

Me: No, it's not. I started the whole thing.
William: No, it was me.

I frown at William:

"Dude, what are you saying?"

And before I can react, (it's happening too often today), Justine steps forward.

Justine: No, it was me.

One after the other, my friends step forward and say:

Max: No, it was me.
Benjamin: No, it was me.
Vanessa: No, it was me.
Chloé C.: No, it was me.
Sabrina: No, it was me.
Tommy (!!!!): No, it was me.

Uh, I can't remember his name (He's tall and slim, and always wears a red baseball cap. He has a Russian name, or something like that.)

Anyway, him: No, it was me. (Light Russian accent)

AMAZING!! JUST LIKE A MOVIE SCENE!!
(Even one of Kevin's guys felt like stepping forward.
But he changed his mind, just in case...)

Mrs. Diane stares at us all without understanding what's going on. She grabs Kevin by the arm.

Mrs. D: You're headed straight to the director's office.
Kevin: What!? And not him!? (pointing at William)
Mrs. D: You too, William!

I try to interfere, but William blocks my way. He says:

William: It's okay.

Me: ???????
William: I have been waiting for this moment for a long time.

I watch them leave.

without knowing what to say.

Me: ...
Me: ... (towards Max, shrugging)
Me: ... (towards Justine, shrugging)
Justine: ... (towards me, shrugging)
Me: ... (towards... no one)
Max: ... (he also shrugs)

We all stared at each other without saying a word before heading back to our classes.

I DIDN'T SEE WILLIAM FOR THE REST OF THE DAY. NOR KEVIN.

School will be closed for two weeks for the Holidays.
DARN.

(I mean, I'm happy that the Holidays are finally here, but I am wondering what's happening with William.)

As soon as I get home, I ask mom for the school DIRECTORY.

Mom: Why?
Me: I need a phone number.

Mom: Who's?
Me: No one.
Mom: No one?

** I admit. I make no sense, but there's NO WAY I am telling her who or why.

AAARGH! She's staring with those witch's eyes... I am weakening.

Me: I mean... someone.
Mom (Hands on the hips): Someone?

AAARGH! How is that her business!?

Note to self: In my new country, kids will be able to keep secrets from their parents... and moms with sorcerer's diplomas will be banned or imprisoned! No magic allowed!

I am not telling her.

LONG ENDLESS PAUSE...

But her gaze intensifies. Her **black magic** is powerful, and getting to my brains. I must **fight it**.

OOPH. I mustn't tell her. **OOPH**... But she's a sorcerer. The real deal. She's hypnotizing, and I am completely **under her spell**.

AAAAAARGH!!!!

Me: William Thompson.

Mom: ???

<u>Her reaction can mean two things:</u>

> 1) She doesn't know who William is.
> 2) She knows him, but doesn't know why I would need to speak to him.

Mom: William Thompson? Why?
Me: Can't I call him if I want to?
Mom: Why would you want to?

> *P.S.* ****** I hesitate, but because it's for a **good cause**, I shouldn't worry.

Me: I want to thank him for today.

Mom considers me for A SECOND, but she believes me. She gets the directory.

10 minutes later...
(**Sitting in the basement, with my hands sweaty.)

Mrs. Thompson: Hello?
Me: Hello, may I speak to William Thompson, please?
**

WILLIAM THOMPSON?? Seriously??

Mrs. Thompson: He hasn't arrived yet.
Me: Really? It's so late?
Mrs. Thompson: I know. I tried to call him but he's not answering.
Me: ...
Mrs. Thompson: Who's talking?
Me: Er... it's... no one...

SERIOUSLY?

Me: Er... I'll call back later... thanks.

I hang up so quickly I don't even know if she said anything. I should have told her what happened today... but it's not my business to discuss this with her.

AND MAYBE WILLIAM DOESN'T WANT TO TALK ABOUT IT WITH HIS MOM?

Come think of it, the school will probably call his

parents to explain what happened. I should have given my **side of the story**, so that William doesn't get in trouble with his parents. I know I would.

In my bed that night, I think about what happened. I really hope William is okay, and that Kevin + *HIS 3 STOOGES* didn't get him back after school.

Trying to keep up...

Much later that evening...

It's *11:11PM.* (I make a wish... I always do when all the numbers are the same on the clock...)

I can't stop thinking about William. I really hope he's fine.

December 25th
I watch the beautiful snow falling slowly on the street. It's wonderful.

I looooove Christmas, especially when it snows! We played outside for many hours (even Melia had fun ~~with us~~).

Then mom made hot chocolate, and we opened our presents. It was great, even if I received only **5** of the **17 presents** I had asked for (better luck next year, I guess).

<u>Note to self:</u> I should offer to walk Shivers for mom more often...

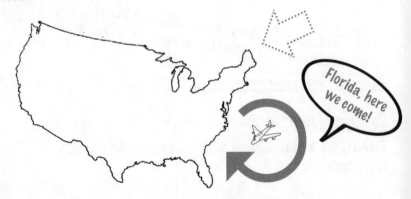

December 29th

*On the beach, IN FLORIDA – the twins are having fun building a sand castle. I play with them... It's kind of fun, even if it's cold outside.

We arrived in Florida a few days ago. I am sending Max **an email**.

To: max3875@(secret!!).com
From: Charlie4428@(secret!!).com
Hey Max,
Any news from William or the others?
Charlie

To: Charlie4428@(secret!!).com
From: max3875(secret!!).com
Hey Charlie,
No, I am stuck going to family parties and I am bored. You?

(**BTW** my uncle Frankie was drunk again last night, and he cracked his skull open after tripping in the stairs. There was blood EVERYWHERE... AWESOME!!!!)

Max

MAX loves to give such details...

Later, that same day...

I hope William is okay. I can't stop thinking about talking to him.

To say thank you. Hm, bigger: **thank you**.

** That's better!

It's not exaggerating to say he saved my life. He's **really not** a *LOOOOSER*.

P.S. ** I told my cousin what happened, and he says he wouldn't have punched Kevin. Just because he hates fights.

The more I look at him, the less I think he's fat.

** I'm talking about William, not Joje.

P.P.S. ** He's a little **CHUBBY**. Er, I mean... **CURVACEOUS, IT'S MORE POLITE**.

P.P.S. ** I'll ask mom to make

CARAMEL BROWNIES FOR HIM, he will like them. He loves sugar!! He always has two desserts for lunch... except when they serve **PUDDING**.

Then he takes THREE PORTIONS!!

I love pudding.

Me too.

December 31st

**In the ocean – not for long because the water's really cold.

I swam all day (not true – for 20 minutes only) with Joje in the ocean. He and his family are also here... It's totally cool!

P.S. ** Not that I want to be annoying, but I really hope that William is okay.

January 1st

**Our parents are still sleeping, although it's 9:58AM. They celebrated New Year's last night and went to bed late. I'm hungry. I will wake mom up at 10AM.

It's raining, and there's nothing interesting to do. Mom and Aunt Steffy have a hangover, so they don't feel like doing anything.

I don't know where this obsession is coming from, but I really hope that Kevin will leave William **ALONE**. William never **provokes Kevin**. He doesn't deserve it.

January 3rd

On the sofa, at the condo.

Still raining. We went to the movies and saw the most **booooooring** film **EVER**. Another animation, because that's all the twins like to watch. But there was nothing else playing, so we didn't have a choice. Even the popcorn had too much SALT IN IT. **Disgusting**.

I can't remember. Was William going away somewhere during the Holidays?

A bit later, after thinking a lot about it...
He probably did. He and his parents always travel around the world when they can.

I discussed my "country" project with Joje. He loves the idea, and would really like to help me find a cool name for it.

Here are a few POSSIBILITIES:

1) Zombieland. I know, I know, I have mentioned it before, but this is the "official" list.
2) NO RULES. Joje's idea. Can't say I really like it.
3) TOTALLY COOL. Not bad for a country name!
4) PARTY TIME. Very cool, but not so serious.
5) We should create a name with the first syllable of each one of our names... AWESOME IDEA!!

- If Joje doesn't agree, **too bad.**
My country, my idea, **My decision.**

He mentioned writing a charter with laws. Not a bad idea. We can do that after we find a name.

P.S. ** Once again, Joje doesn't agree with me. He says we should do that **BEFORE** finding a name. He always has to have the final say everything, and that really bugs me.
(Can't wait for the holidays to be over).

** I am the **PRESIDENT AND PRIME MINISTER,**
I should be deciding.

P.P.S. ** Is he maybe right? We'll see...

January 4th
Getting off the plane... or almost!

We came back home late at night –
at around 1am! **MOM** finally let me go to bed late ;-)
= so today is really **January 5th.**

SCHOOL TOMORROW.

I can say tomorrow because it is after midnight, so we are already tomorrow. Right? Hmm... very confusing... and there's no jetlag!

> ** I should maybe call William to find out if he had fun during the holidays... and I could wish him a **HAPPY NEW YEAR.**

> *P.P.S.* ** No use. I will see him tomorrow.

January 6th
(Everywhere in school, even **dark places I never go to.)

I looked for William everywhere** this morning when I got to school, but I couldn't find him. He's not in school today. **(That or he's in the best hiding place in the whole school!)** Didn't see Kevin either. Not that I looked for him.

The minute I get home, I call his place. **(When I finally find the courage to call, of course)**.

Mrs Thompson: Hello?
Me: Hello, may I speak with Thompson please?

DID I JUST SAY THAT... AGAIN!?!
THOMPSON??? I CAN'T BE THAT NERVOUS???

Mrs. Thompson: I'm sorry, William's not well.
Who's speaking?
Me: Er... it's –

click = Someone else gets on the line.

William (weird voice): Hello?
Mrs. Thompson and Me: William?
William (weird voice): It's okay, mom. You can hang up.
Mrs. Thompson: Don't talk too much, sweetie.
William (weird voice): MOM?!? HANG UP THE PHONE!!

click = she's out.

William (weird voice): Hello?
Me: Hello?
William (weird voice): Who's there?
Me: Hi William, it's Charlie. Charles. Charlie.

William (weird voice): Hi Charlie, how are you?
Me (~~weird voice~~): What's wrong with your voice?
William (weird voice): I have tonsillitis... That's why I didn't go to school today. I won't go tomorrow either.
Me: And Wednesday?
William (weird voice): I don't know. I guess so.
Me: I'm sorry for you...
William (weird voice): Don't worry about it, it's cool. I can eat only ice cream.

OF COURSE!!!

Me: Cool... and candy, I guess?
William: ???

I realize I just said something stupid. He can't eat **candy**, only ice cream, because of his sore throat!!
(= Ice cream is cold so it helps with the swelling in the throat)

Me: ...
William: ...
Me: Oh, my sister wants to play.

William: ???
Me: Gotta go. Bye!

As I hang up (quite fast), I realize I forgot to thank him. *DAMN!* Maybe he doesn't remember?

P.S. ** **much later** (At around 9:08pm
– I just went to bed)
** Of course he remembers.

At school.

As soon as I see William, I walk over to him at his locker. He is by himself, as usual.

*Kevin is still not there

Me (shy): Hey William...
William (happy to see me): Hey Charlie!
Me: Feeling better?
William: A bit, yeah.
Me: Listen, I wanted to th----

Max arrives...

Max (To William): Hey fatso!

{ To myself = fatso?? We NEVER call him that to his face?? }

Max (To me): What are you doing talking to him?
Me: Er

My eyes cross William's, and he's clearly hurt. I am really uncomfortable, and I don't know what to say. After *TOO MANY SECONDS* of awkwardness, William breaks the silence.

William (To Max): Don't worry, Max, we weren't talking. Charles was looking for you.

William stares hard at me for a long time before Max grabs my arm to leave. I am very uncomfortable, and my throat is tight. **weird**.

I feel bad **ALL** morning...

I can't stop seeing his eyes staring at me. He seemed sad... or disappointed, even, that I left with Max. But Max is my best friend, William should understand that.

P.S. *** In the pm. Miss Howard comes to my desk to talk to me.

Miss Howard: Are you alright, Charles?

** Not that I don't like my name, but I prefer being called

CHARLIE.

Me: Yes. Why?
Miss Howard: You seem... very far away, today. You are not focussed.
Me: ...

NO IDEA what to say to this. I'm most certainly not going to say: « Yes, very far away, and not listening to a word you're saying! » I'd have to be REALLY STUPID.

Miss Howard: You know what to do for your homework?
Me: Um... yes.

She turns around to speak to the whole class. Good. She believes me.

Miss Howard: Don't hesitate if something is not clear for tomorrow.

P.S. ** I have far more important things to deal with before understanding the homework. I need to thank William.

At lunch

At the cafeteria. Usual table with my friends.

William is sitting by himself, as usual. He's eating his lunch, looking at his plate without looking up. He looks at no one, and no one is paying any attention to him.

THE USUAL...

I can't stop looking in his direction. But he doesn't look up once.

Tension is building up...

That night It's about *7:27PM*

Mom walks into my room to make sure everything's alright.
(There she goes again.)

Me: Yeah, why?
Mom: You look distracted.
Me: ...
Mom: Is something bothering you at school?

AMAZING! my mom is not just a witch, she's also **clairvoyant!**

I didn't realize it showed so much that I'm thinking about William. I didn't speak much at dinner, but then again, I never do much because Lulu usually takes the stage (she's cute, but has nothing interesting to say).

Me (I shrug): ...
Mom: Does it have anything to do with Thompson?

{ **What!?! How does she know?! I have to pick my jaw up from the floor.** }

I know everything. He he...

Me: _!!!_

She ~~seats~~ sits next to me.

Mom: You never spoke to him for five years, and yet you called him before Christmas to thank him. For what, exactly?
Me: Nothing.

None of her business, and I won't say anything.

Mom: Charlie, if you don't tell me, I won't be able to help you...

OH NOoo! She's doing it again with that crazy look. She's too strong for me. Less than *30 SECONDS* later, I told her everything = spaghetti sauce + pump (asthma) + ~~JUSTINE~~ (no idea why I mentioned HER) + hum, his - well deserved - fist in Kevin's face.

Mom: Is she cute?

WHAT!?! THAT'S _VERY_ AWKWARD!!! **NO way** I am telling my mom anything about Justine!!

AAAARGH!

Me: Of everything I just told you, that's all you picked up on??

Mom: You never tell me anything. Happy to know you're interested in girls.
Me: Er... **ABSOLUTELY NOT!!!** Can we focus on the important stuff please?

Is she cute, yes, or no?

Here we go! Here are her suggestions for what I should do: "You should give him a chance" blah blah blah... "Maybe it's his way of showing that he wants to be your friend." blah blah blah... "He seems like a nice boy..." blah blah blah!

Me: But mom?!? He's the biggest loooser at school!! What will people say?
Mom: The ones who laugh or tease don't deserve your friendship. And if Max doesn't understand, well, that's too bad for him. You don't need to justify yourself to anyone... except me, of course.

{HMM....I GUESS SO...}

Me: How do I do it?
Tutu: Oh! It's easy!!

We both **jump**. Tutu is standing at the door and heard everything. He always spies on me and I never hear him!

Me: What are you doing there?
Tutu: Um... I'm listening.

And who appears from behind him? **The sheep!** My sister Lulu, and she laughs out loud.

Lulu: Me toooooooooooo!!!!! Jus-tiiiiine, Jus-tiiii-ne.

> **I want to kill her... not for real, of course, but I am really **mad**.

Me: Get out of my room, you brats!!
Mom: Charlie, calm down!
Lulu: Jus-tiiiiine!!!
Mom: Lulu, that's enough! Go to the living room window and tell me when dad gets home.
Tutu (head down): No sense of humour in this house.
Me: Stop it!!
Mom: Charlie! Let it go! **(to the twins)** I said: downstairs!!

They obey right away.
> **Can't blame them. I would have as well...

Mom goes on...

Mom: Only you can know, Charles. When the time is right, you'll know it and you'll be able to seize the opportunity to thank him.

GOOD POINT, Mrs. Witch.

That night

It's *7:46 PM* – Oh! I mean, it's now *7:47 PM*!

This whole "William" thing is driving me nuts! Why can't I just forget about it and get on with my life?!?

To: joje@(secret).com
From: Charlie4428@(secret).com
Hey Joje,
Should I be friends with William? What would you do if you were me?
Charlie

To: Charlie4428@(secret).com
From: joje@(secret).com
It's your decision, cousin. But no matter what, you should thank him. What he did for you... then time will tell.
Joje

He's right. He always has the right thing to say to me. That's normal, he's older than me.

EIGHT MONTHS IS A LOT AT OUR AGE. MOM ALWAYS SAYS SO.

WHAT?!?

Just go to bed, Charles.

January 15th (in class)

Kevin's back in school today. He was suspended for a week. Too bad for him. From what I hear, if he bullies anyone again, he will be expelled for good.

Yikes.

Not cool for him, if he has to leave school...
But veeeeeery cool for us. He deserves it!!

** I am at the cafeteria.

Sitting at "my" table, as usual, at the end of it, near the aisle. (It's spaghetti day, and everyone is eating it because it's soooo good!!)

William has to walk by my table in order to get to his in the back of the room. He's walking, his plate in his hands, and minding his own business. But he has to walk by Kevin's table ... who stands up to block his way. *IDIOT #1* + *IDIOT #2* + *IDIOT #3* imitate him, as usual. *OH OH*, every one knows what's coming...

> We all turn to watch = No one is breathing and you could hear a pin drop.

Kevin really has bad judgement, defying the principal's orders to leave William alone.

William: Let me by, please.
>> **I would never have said « please ».
William is too polite.

Kevin: What are you going to do to me? Huh? You can't hit me, both your hands are holding your plate. Stupid fat ass.
>> **Wow, he's lucky my mom's not here because she would have a fit over his language.

111

William looks down. He clearly doesn't want any trouble, and I can't blame him. <u>But I know what's coming:</u> William's plate will fly to the floor, thanks to Kevin.

****I AM RAGING. THIS IS UNFAIR.****

Without thinking, I stand up, walk up to William and grab his plate.

Me (To Kevin): Not anymore. **(To William)** Do what you have to do, we're all behind you. Me first.

AWKWARD... BUT AWESOME!!

** BTW, my voice was firm and defiant. For once, I feel like a super hero, even if I'm shaking inside. But I'm so cool! ☺☺☺

William is as surprised as Kevin, and as... well... ME!!

I go back to my table with the plate. Mrs Diane arrives at the same moment, but William followed me.

Instead of giving him his plate back, I put it on the table, at the seat next to mine.

MAX IS PALE.

William looks at me, not sure of what to do. I invite him to sit next to me with a nod.

William (hesitating): You sure?
Me: Why wouldn't I be?
William: Well, um... I don't know...
Me: Well, ... sit down!

He's still hesitating. As if he thinks I would humiliate him once he's sitting. (I would **NEVER** do that. I can't believe I even mentioned it.)

EXCEPT **FOR MELIA.**
I HAVE NO PROBLEM HUMILIATING HER.

Me: Come on! Sit down... before I eat your plate!!!

We all **LAUGH** because we know William will **NEVER** let me eat his plate without a fight!

**Kevin looks at me with KILLER EYES. I'll have to be careful over the next few days... **

I turn around: JUSTINE watched the whole thing and she is looking at me... with a huge smile on her face. I flush, and my legs are shaky.

Later that night...

It's about 7:14PM.

We just finished another family dinner. Lulu told us about her boring day, in boring detail.

The phone rings.

Probably Simon = Melia and him are back together for the HUNDREDTH TIME. I stopped counting, especially since he found out she likes Nick.

She made peace with Nana. After all, it's a compliment that your BFF finds your boyfriend cute. Doesn't mean she wants to date him.

At least that's what she wrote in her diary. I was at that part when mom busted me, so I don't exactly know how it ended. But no worries, I'll find out next time... ;-)

Good luck with that!

MY LIFE

It takes Melia **three pages** to explain a *TWO SECOND EVENT*. But I've already established that she has a **lot of time on her hands**.

I am on FACETIME with JOJE.
It's about **8:14pm** – In my bed, under my comforter.

Joje: You're kidding?
Me: No! He sat with us!
Joje: So he will sit with you guys everyday from now on?
Me: Of course! He's like, my friend now!
Joje: Charlie, you're sooooo cool!
Me: I don't know about that, but I'm really happy.

I don't tell him about Justine. I don't see how mentioning her would be relevant to this story. I mean, other people were there as well, and I'm not talking about them.

Me: One thing's for sure, I feel much better!! Oh! have you thought of some names for our country??
Joje: Not really...

Me: We should hurry, before someone else steals our idea.
Joje (Frowning. **I see him, thanks to FaceTime**): ...

Okay. That was a stupid remark. I don't know what to say.

***Mom walks in with the telephone.

Me: Gotta go.
Joje: Ciao.
Me (To Mom): What is it?

She hands me the device.

Mom: It's for you. It's Max.
Me (grabbing the phone): Thanks. Can you close the door behind you?

I WAIT FOR HER TO LEAVE.

Me: Hi Max!
Max: Hey.
Me: What's up?
Max: You didn't answer my email?
Me: I didn't see it...
Max: Call me back after reading it.
Me: We're talking! Tell me now!
Max: Well... um...
Me: What?
Max: Is William going to sit with us all the time now?

I get dizzy. **Why** is he asking this question? He's my **best friend**. He should know that I don't like to see William getting bullied.

TOO BAD FOR HIM.

{ And I just told Joje William was my friend now. I can't change my mind. And I won't. }

So what if William's a bit... bigger than average**??**

It's not his fault if he eats *ALL THE TIME*. Max better not ask me to choose between him or William, because I will choose William.

After hesitation...

Me: You have a problem with that?
Max: No. Just wanted to know. You did well today, Charlie.

Phiiiiieeeeew!!!!

I really didn't feel like choosing.

** Thank God!!**

Me: He's cool.
Max: Yeah. I guess he can step up if Kevin annoys us.
Me: Yup! He sure knows how to throw a punch, that's for sure!
Max: Might as well have him on our side!!!

We laughed and agreed to see each other the next day.

Mom made the caramel brownies like I asked her. She's **nice**. Strict, but **nice**.

January 17th

We're in class, and the bell rings and school lets out. We all put our things away.

Miss Howard: Don't forget the homework for tomorrow. Have a great evening! Charles, can you come here for a minute?

UH-OH...

To myself: What did I do now??

Only mom can punish me for Melia.

Max gives me a thumb-up, and William, a tap on the back. I fake a smile, but I just want to throw up. No one likes to be called to the teacher's desk. I'm no exception.

P.S. ** I love Miss Howard. She's really the coolest! But I'd rather NOT be called to her desk. (especially not in front of the whole class – it should be illegal). I could have done better on the math test (or English??), I'll do better next time, promise.

I walk up to her desk.

**Much slower than usual, I must admit.

Me: ...

(I keep silent: she should start talking, right?)

Miss Howard: I know what you did for William the other day at the cafeteria.
Me: ...

Er... OKay. I know it too!?! (Duh, I was there!)

Miss Howard smiles at me.

Miss Howard: I am very proud of what you did. William came to see me and he's really happy. Thank you Charles.

** I don't know why, but I feel like... crying. Of joy, of course. It's nice to make people happy, RIGHT?

I like making people happy!

I like making people sleepy.

February 1st

At school = class + cafeteria + gymnasium + playground

Things are smooth between William, Max and I. We call each other the three musketeers. Tommy is jealous. Too bad for him. That's life, like mom would say. Justine and I talk a lot... well, more than before, anyway. She's cool, you know, for a girl. Back to William, he's hilarious. He makes me laugh out loud, and I really like spending time with him.

He's the BEST impersonator in the world. He can imitate singers, actors, and even female celebrities, but we promised we wouldn't tell anyone.

I don't believe it! We've been in the same class for five years and we didn't really speak to each other before now!!

P.S. ** Same thing happened with a guy in Joje's class. They were together for 6 years before they became friends. (I don't remember the guy's name though, Stephen, maybe?) but this new friend wasn't bullied, so it's not the same as William. It's pretty cool, to make new friends, and my cousin agrees with me on this. I should introduce him to Max and William, I am sure they would get along.

February 15th

In my room, on my bed. It's **6PM** sharp. I should make a wish, even if I usually do only when all the numbers are the same (e.g.: 3:33pm or 4:44pm)

Max and I are invited to William's house tomorrow to play and hang out. *COOL*. The **THREE MUSKETEERS** will get to spend the whole day together. I'll bring William a pan of caramel brownies.

** I shout, to make sure mom can hear me from the kitchen.

ME: MOM??? Can you bake caramel brownies for William, please?

I think she said YES. We'll see later. I can't wait to go! I don't know where William lives, but he mentioned he has all the latest video games consoles! He's an only child. **lucky him**.

There is a knock on my door.

**I ROLL MY EYES...

Me: Who is it?
Tutu: It's Tutu.
Me: What do you want?
Tutu: To come in!?!

I roll my eyes again. He's so annoying. But I know that if I don't let him, he will bug me until I do, so I might as well do so and save me the frustration.

Me: Come in.

He opens the door and walks in.

Tutu: What are you doing?

He "sings" when he talks and it's really irritating. And he's got the most annoying high pitch voice...

Me: None of your business.

123

Tutu: Oh...

Me: ...

Tutu: (He looks around to try to figure out what I am doing.)

I hid my notebook under my pillow. Don't want him to get his hands on it and read it.

Me (impatient): what do you want?

Tutu: Mom says it's time for dinner.

GRRRRRRRRRRR... And she couldn't call me herself and save me the trouble?

Me: Next time, go bother Granny!

OH DARN...

(My sister Melia goes nuts when I call her granny - and Tutu ALWAYS tells on me.)

His eyes bug out and he shouts:

Tutu: MOM!?! CHARLIE JUST CALLED MELIA Granny!

TRAITOR. I HATE HIM.

Melia's voice (from the hallway): Aaargh!!!! I'm going to kill you!

Mom's voice (from the kitchen): Stop fighting and come eat, NOW!

But Melia storms into my room and jumps on my bed (she's hitting me hard). *UH OH...*

Melia: I said: STOP CALLING ME THAT!

ME: OUCH!! You're hurting me!!!

*DAD WALKS IN***.

** I didn't know he was back from work already.

Dad: What's going on here? Melia, leave your brother alone!
Melia: He started it!
Me: Not true!
Tutu: True!
Me: You, mind your own business!
Dad: Tutu, go downstairs. **(Tutu leaves)** And you two! Just stop it! I'm getting sick of these arguments and fights. I've had enough!
Me: It's her fault! And she's not even my real sister!

UH OH, dad's really not happy now. I really should have kept quiet.

I hate to get mad, but they leave me no choice.

Dad: Don't ever say that again or else you won't go to your friend's house tomorrow. Are we clear?

Nooooo! That would be the end of my life... uh, so to speak. I have no choice but to fold.

Me: Crystal clear.

I won't say another word all night.

JUST IN CASE I SAY SOMETHING INCRIMINATING.

Dad: Now apologize to each other.
Melia: No way! He should be the one apologizing!
Dad: I don't want to hear it! You will both apologie, or else you are both grounded all night. No dinner.
Me: ?!?

What?!? Since when did he get so strict?!?

Melia: ...

I really want to go to William's tomorrow.

Me: I'm sorry.
Melia (not sincere)**:** Sorry.
Dad (to Melia – eh eh)**:** Do it properly.
Melia (crossing her arms)**:** ...
Dad: Do it now!
Melia (uncrossing her arms)**:** I'm sorry.

HMM... **She sounded** sincere.

Dad's happy. So am I... I guess. We all go downstairs.

And so they love each other, again.

Thanks to me!

The following day...

What a great day! William is the funniest, he is soooo different from before!

FIRST OF ALL, his house is like a castle. We decided to watch **HORROR MOVIES** instead of playing video games. He loooooves **HORROR** movies, and his parents let him watch them as many times as he wants. *SOOOOO COOL!!*

Horror movies scare me.

We saw three:

HALLOWEEN, HALLOWEEN II AND PSYCHO.

SICK !!!

It was like a **HORROR MOVIE FESTIVAL**. I have to say, I had my eyes closed half the time, but I had an idea of what was going on.

I never close my eyes!

And the nanny let us eat in front of the television. Mom **NEVER** lets us.

P.S. ****** William's nanny doesn't speak a word of English. She's from somewhere in Asia. We can say ANYTHING we want and she won't **understand a thing!**

So Max and I enjoyed it very much. Our moms are the worst, and they never let us do anything. Well, my mom is the worst... But we ate commercial frozen lasagna. At least my mom cooks better. She actually cooks. Period.

{ ****** I almost threw up when William joked the lasagna was made with human blood. I could taste the blood, almost. First and last time I was eating frozen lasagna. My mom always prepares it from scratch, and it's awesome. }

We ate a frozen McCain cake for desert. I must convince mom to buy one, they are **AMAZING**. After all that, we had **popcorn with M&M's**. That's right! William throws M&M's in his popcorn.

I completely disagree.

IT'S SICK!!! It's a mixture of sweet and salty **CRAZY AWESOMENESS!** From now on, I'll never have popcorn without M&M's!!

We also founded a **three musketeers club**. We haven't figured out what we'll do with it, but we'll see.

Didn't the three musketeers have a dog?

The day went by too quickly. William's really the nicest. Max as well, but I knew that already. William invited me to his cottage for school break. It's in the mountains, about two hours north from here, and we'll go skiing. **COOL!!!** I can't wait to go.

I have wanted to ski there for a while, but my parents say it's too far from our house. And they say it's a bit expensive. You know, with four kids and all. But it doesn't matter, it's just nice that we can ski.

IT'S TOO BAD Max won't be there, we could have worked on our three musketeers club. Max doesn't ski, and he hates it.

Hopefully, mom will agree to this. I swear, if she doesn't, I don't know what I'm going to do. Uh...

I'll go on a HUNGER STRIKE. Yup. That's what I'll do!!

A HUNGER STRIKE. My mom's going to TOTALLY FREAK OUT.

Later in the day:
**Before dinner – At the house, in the kitchen.

Me: Mom?

Mom: Yes, honey?

Me: Er... well... um... you know, William?

Mom: I'm so glad you guys are friends. He's a really nice boy.

Me: Yup... He has a cottage in the mountains.

Mom: Oh! That's nice!

Me: Um... well... he sort of... well... he invited me to spend a few days up there during school break. To ski.

Mom: Really?

Me: Hmm... (My ten fingers are crossed... please, please, pleeeeease, say yessssssssssss.)

Mom: Um...

** She's about to say **no**, as usual. That's it! I'll start a hunger strike tomorrow morning, um... I mean tomorrow night... uh... right after dinner.

P.S. ** I'll eat more beforehand...
so I can last longer.

Mom: Okay.

Me: Whaaaat???????

Mom (surprised? confused?): What, you don't want to?

Me: No, I mean yes! It's just that... I didn't think that...

... You're usually such a bummer.

Me: Cool! You're okay with it?

Mom: But let me call his mom first just to make sure it's alright... Okay?

Me: Sure.

DOUBLE COOL, I will eat **A HUGE CHOCOLATE SUNDAE** for dessert!! Hurray!! No hunger strike for Charlie!!!

* * *11 SECONDS LATER* * *

I am **SOOOOOOO** sending William an e-mail <u>tonight</u> to give him the good news!

P.S. ** My cousin Joje will be jealous. Skiing is his favorite sport.

Two weeks later...

It's the eve of my trip to William's cottage! I am almost done with my luggage when mom walks in.

Mom: Here. The rest of your ski clothes. You'll wear your helmet, right?
Me: Of course!

Mom (she doesn't seem to believe me...): Promise me.
There are so many accidents.
I can't stop you from going fast, but if you wear a
helmet, it'll reassure me. And it can save your life,
you know.

Me: I know, mom. Don't worry. Anyway, I know
William will wear his.

Mom: Even if he didn't, I would want you to wear
yours.

Me: I got it, mom. I'll wear the helmet. Did you make
the cupcakes?

Tutu: Yes, she did... And we can have one, Lulu and I.

****Geez**, I hadn't seen him! He's standing in the door
to my room, and he's listening to our conversation.

Cupcakes are actually my favo-rites... if anyone cares...

Me: What are you doing there?
Tutu: Nothing.

YEAH, RIGHT?!?!

Mom: Tutu, go read in your room, please.

He moans, but obeys without arguing. Good idea.

I'll say.

Mom: You'll bring a bottle of wine for his dad.
And I got a little something for his mom.
Me: You're so cool.
Mom: You bet I'm cool!!!

She kisses me on the forehead before leaving my room.

NOT COOL.

I CAN'T WAIT FOR TOMORROW!

Max and his family have gone to his grandparents' place. He wrote me that he's bored with his family and that he would prefer to be with us at the cottage.

I am SOOOOOO bringing my ~~diar~~ notebook **I want to remember everything!**

P.S. ** Come to think of it, it's pretty cool to write in a ~~diar~~ notebook. But I must make sure Melia – and nobody else, either - finds it. That's why I hide it under my... er... my... nowhere...

10 pm

I'm writing because I can't sleep = tooooooo **excited!**

Mom: Charlie, go to bed, You're going to be tired in the morning.
Me: Yeah yeah...

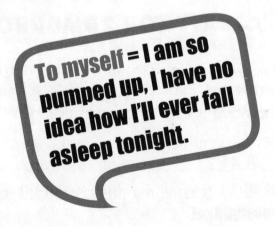

To myself = I am so pumped up, I have no idea how I'll ever fall asleep tonight.

I finally slip under my sheets.

I open my eyes. *YIPPEE!* The night is finally over!

I look at the clock. *5:14 AM. SHOOT!*

It's way too early.

I close my eyes.

I open my eyes an hour later (or so I think)... *5:18 AM.*

WHAT?!? Only **four minutes** went by?? That's

CRAZY!!!

I try to get back to sleep... then I wake up again...
8:24 AM? **WHAT!?!** I didn't hear the alarm! I have
to hurry up and shower really fast. William and his
mom will be here in *35 MINUTES!*

Me (I shout): MOM????????
Mom (from the other room): What?
Me (Grabbing my clothes in a hurry so I can get into the shower. I open my door and rush to the bathroom): Why didn't you wake me up before?
Mom: I was just about to.
Me (I roll my eyes. No time for foolish behaviour...): ...

I turn the door knob, but the door is locked.

Me: Meliaaaaaaaa! Hurry up, I'm in a rush!
Melia (through the door): You should've woken up earlier! Wait for your turn.

I AM FUMING.

Me: Moooooom! Melia's pissing me off!!
(Oops, that came out wrong)

P.S. ** I know I am in trouble when I see my mom's eyes bug out. THE WITCH IS TOTALLY "WITCHING" RIGHT NOW, and she scares me.

Mom: What did you say?

Me (taking the Fifth): …
Mom: What kind of language is that?
Me: Sorry. I meant: She's giving me a hard time.

> **To myself** = Since when do I say that?

Me: I'm going to be late!
Mom (knocking on the door): Melia, can you hurry up, please?
Melia (shouts once more): I JUST GOT IN!! And I'm having some problems, so he'll have to wait his turn.

P.S. ** Her "problem" is probably a pimple she can't get rid of because:
A) it's huge;
B) it hurts (well, that's what she says);
C) it's in between layers of skin (so she says).

MOM TURNS TO ME.

Mom: Use my bathroom. I don't want the Thompsons to wait for you.
Me: Thanks.

P.S. ** I am NEVER allowed to use my parents' bathroom. It's, like, sacred in there. And now that I'm here, I can't enjoy it because I have to hurry. unfair.

So rolling my eyes, right now.

Three minutes later:
(For real, it's 8:39am = 15 minutes later)

I rush out of the shower and run downstairs for breakfast. COOL!!!

Mom made French toast. **MY FAVOURITE!**
(** Amongst other things)

Handing me a plate

Mom: You're going to call me tonight?
Me (mouth full): Hmm...
Mom: I'll call Helen anyway (William's mom). I have the number.
Me (rolling my eyes): ...
Mom: Hey! I saw that!
Me: What?!? How??

P.S. ** This woman really freaks me out.

Mom: I see EVERYTHING.

YOU'RE TELLING ME!!!

Mrs. Witch! She doesn't miss a thing. *EVER.*

Me: YESSSSSSSSS!!!

FINALLY, ALONE FOR A FEW DAYS!!! FOR THREE WHOLE DAYS!! HEAVEN ON EARTH!!!

I go back up to my room to get my backpack.

Tutu: Where are you going?

Me: You know where! To William's cottage.
Tutu: But to do what?

AAARRRGH! He's so annoying!

Me: I have to go, they're waiting for me downstairs.
Tutu: I'm going to miss you.

I freeze. Aww, that's a really nice thing to say to his older brother. He wants a hug.

NO WAY!!!

Okay. A small one. To make him happy. I'll make it quick.

Lulu (in the frame of my bedroom door): I want a hug too!

OOOOOH, hadn't seen her there!

Me (she's so adorable...): Ah! Okay. Come here, but make it quick!

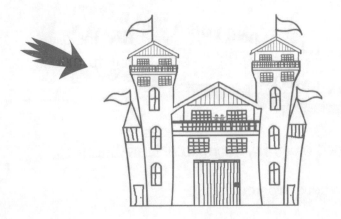

OMG!!!

That's not a **cottage**, it's a **CASTLE!!!** Almost as big as *AS BUCKINGHAM PALACE!***. Okay, not so much, but close enough...

William's cottage is on a lake, near the ski slopes.

**AMAZING!!!

P.S. ** I was born in the wrong family.

I must convince my parents to buy a cottage! There are so many things to do here!! At William's they have a pool table, a ping-pong table and a pinball machine! It's all in the mega cool basement, and they have a bar, where we can make ourselves hot chocolate with

LOADS OF MARSHMALLOWS!!!

They also have a **popcorn** machine like the ones you see in movie theaters. I **SOOOOOO** want to move here!!

His mom made spaghetti sauce with meatballs (not as good as mom's, and it doesn't look homemade) with a Cæsar salad (bottled dressing = Definitely not as good as mom's). My mom makes the best one in the world.

William's parents didn't have dinner with us. They had dinner much later, while we were playing downstairs. William tells me they never eat all together as a **family**. That's so different than my reality. Mom **insists** that we all eat together every night:

NIGHTMARE!

We skied all day and it was great because the weather was perfect. Not too cold outside. Then we watched **FRIDAY THE 13TH**, parts 1 and 2. We also had **popcorn with M&M's**. I love it, it's crazy!!

No comment.

P.S. ** Never going back home.
EVER!!

We did many other things, but I'd rather not write, because... well I don't want to get in trouble...

P.S. ** Joje will go nuts when I tell him about my weekend. He has the right to know. **Ha ha.**

That evening...

I don't know what time it is exactly because there is no clock in the guest room. Weird. This house has everything, except for clocks!

WOW... William's mom is ~~quite the babe~~ um, very beautiful. She's almost intimidating. And her legs...

Wow. They go up to here!!! OOPH. Hard to believe William is her biological son, they really don't look alike.

March 4th

In the car, coming back from the dentist. About 12 minutes from my house.

OUCH (= a real OUCH, this time)

Leaving from je denticht I had a cavity that needed treatment.

NIGHTMARE.

I will definitely brush my teech better necht time becavche it hurtch sho much. He had to prick my gumch with a needle and I almosht cried it hurt sho much. All mom shaid wash:

« I told you so!! You never brush your teeth properly! »

Sherioushly?? I am not five yearsh old anymore! But I will make an effort to brush becaushe it hurtsh sho much. And I will shtart floshing...ouch... I can't wait to feel my mouth again.

P.S. ** Slobber's coming out of my mouth and I can't help it. It's gross.

And I'm the sloppy one. Pff!

March 5th

Going up. And down. Up again. And down again.
Going back and forth between the basement and the kitchen
(almost tripped in the stairs on my way down... no joke)

William's coming here for the afternoon. Mom
promised I would have the basement to myself,
and that the twins wouldn't bother us. Melia's gone
to her friend Nana's for two days.

Oops, sorry!
Wrong book.

PEACE AND QUIET! All alone, with my friend,
in the basement, and no annoying twins to bug me.

P.S. ** But the second William stepped foot in the house, the two leeches started bugging us.

Tutu: What are you doing?
Me (rolling my eyes while glancing at William): Nothing. Leave us alone.

Lulu walks up to William with a book.

Lulu: You know this book?
William: No. Sorry, I don't read books for girls.
Lulu: Can I tell you the story?
William (laughs out loud): Er, if you want!

She sits next to him to tell him the story.

Me: Uh, out of the question!! Leave us alone.
Tutu: You're really unkind to your younger siblings.
Me: ...
William: (light smile)

** Up to the kitchen again (No one pays attention to me).

Me: MOOO-OOOMMM!!!!!!!

<u>Back down to the basement, with mom...</u>

AAAAAAAARRRRGHHHH!!!!

No need to say it took half a second for the twins to rush upstairs.

Me: Sorry, they're little brats.
William: No worries. They're so cute.
Me: Whatever... want to play a video game?
William: Okay. But I could use a snack, if it's okay.

OF COURSE!!!!!

Up the stairs once more to get a bag of chips - ooh...
and veggies (I know, it's humiliating, but mom forced me).

SHE REFUSED TO BUY
M&M'S AND POPCORN.

Back down for the last time (hopefully) with *CHIPS*
+ *7-UP...* uh + *VEGGIES* = William smiles. *PHEW.*

We play downstairs all afternoon, until mom calls for
dinner. William reacts when he sees the table.

William: Wow, that's nice!

Joking...

William: Is the pope coming for dinner?
Me: Um... My mom takes family dinners seriously.
Sorry.

Not complaining.

Dad sits at one end of the table. The **twins** walk in as well, and sit at their usual place.

William: Are we... all eating together?
Me: Hmm-mm...... (whispering) She insists we do this every night. She says it's important.
William: Wow...
Lulu: William, come sit next to me!
Me: No!!!
William: Sure! (to me) It's okay.

Pointing at Lulu's doll.

William: Who's that?
Lulu: My doll Caroline. I've had her for a few months, and she wanted to eat with us tonight. I think she likes you.
Me (rolling my eyes): ...
William: Really?

HE LAUGHS!?!

Dad: Tell me, William...**

{ ** Oh gosh. Here we go. A hundred questions from my dad who wants to know everything. God, please don't make him ask stupid questions. He always does that in front of our friends. }

Dad: Do you like Miss Howard?
William: Yeah, she's really cool... I like the year so far. It's my favorite since I started school, especially because we are the Three Musketeers!
Dad: Three musketeers?! Really?!? I guess with Charlie. Who's the other?

(William turns to me.)

William: You didn't tell your parents?
Me (I shrug, what else can I do): ...
William (To my dad): Max.
Dad: Ah! Of course! I should have known!!
William: You really didn't tell your parents??
Me (I shrug, what else can I do): ...

Mom puts the roast beef on the table.

IT SMELLS GREAT!

Mom: He never tells us anything. He likes to play in his room instead.
Tutu: That's true!
Me: Mind your own business!
Lulu: And he's not always nice to us.
Tutu: He's NEVER nice to us!

Lulu: We never do anything, but...
Me: Will you stop it?
Mom: Calm down, Charlie. The twins just want to make conversation with your friend.
Tutu: Charlie told us you had the best house, with games and a marshmallow machine?
Me: It's a popcorn machine! **(lower)** Idiot.

William shrugs but nods while taking a bite.

William: Wow! That's excellent!
Mom: Thanks!
Lulu: If you want to play with Caroline, I could go to your cottage, and we could play together, you know? You can show me how your popcorn machine works. I loooove popcorn.
Tutu: Me tooooooooooooo!!!

I roll my eyes. I'm ashamed of my family.

William (laughs out loud): OK!
Lulu: COOOOOL!!

She looks at me, very proud.

Tutu: For real? I have Lego and Pokemon sticker books. Can I go, too, if I bring them? I'll show you how to play. You're going to love it!
William: I know about Pokemon, I have the whole collection.

Tutu's face drops. William notices and adds...

William: But I haven't bought any in a while, I'm

sure that there are some I don't have. Can you show me?

ER... Why is he so nice to the twins?

Tutu **nods** proudly. He's very happy and turns to me with a huge smile on his face.

William **IS STILL EATING!**

Me: Er... NOT!!! He's just kidding. **(To William)** Pardon them, they're idiots.
Mom: CHARLIE!!
Me: What?!? It's true!
Mom (Severe, and giving me that "witching" look): Don't talk like that.

Me: ☹☹☹

Mom: They're excited because Charlie told us he had so much fun at your place that he wanted to move in!
William: Okay.
Me: Okay?? Okay, what?
William: You can move in if you want.

I look at my parents, **EYES POPPING OUT OF MY HEAD**, and then I turn to William. Seriously!?! Is he really serious??

P.S. ** **SICK!**

William: But if you move into my house, I move in here.
Me: What?!? Oh, no!! Trust me, you DON'T want to move in here!
Mom: Oh really? Why not?
Me: Well, um, well...

❊❊**AWKWARD**

P.S. ❊❊ Sometimes, a good time to shut up comes up, and we miss it. This was that kind of moment.

So, to prove a point, (and to get me out of trouble...), I add...

Me (staring at the witch)**:** What?? It's a nightmare to be bugged by leeches all day long!
William: I'd love to be bugged by my little brother and sister, and have dinner with my family every night. I always have dinner by myself... or with my nanny, and she doesn't speak English.

He bites into a piece of roast beef without looking at us. We stare at him without saying a word.

William: *WOW!* And this is the best meal I've had in years!!
Lulu: My mom's a great cook.

Mom blushes and smiles at Lulu.

I suddenly feel bad, and I'm not so hungry anymore. **William is always** alone at his house. And before we became friends, he was always alone at school also. Being alone all the time can be boring. Maybe that's why he's always constantly eating ... to kill time?

I HAVE SHIVERS JUST THINKING ABOUT IT.

Someone called?

No need to say he wolfed down the Napoleon mom made especially for him.

Mom: Charlie told me it was your favorite.
William: Oh yeah!! That, and chocolate cake... and caramel sundaes... oh, and lemon pie... But I also kind of like crème caramel, that's very good, as well as crème brûlée, but my mom says it's very heavy, so I don't eat it so often... But when I do, I can't have only one!!!

WE ALL START LAUGHING. GEEZ! THAT WILLIAM, I TELL YOU! HE'S A TRUE FOODIE!

It's a bit awkward, because William wants to come to my house all the time now. Even if we don't have all the videos games William has. He says he likes to come here because there's so much life, and it's pretty cool to have brothers and sisters.

P.S. ** I wish I agreed.
** I promise I'll **TRY** to see my family in a more positive light.

I wish I could have brothers and sisters, but only when I felt like it. And when I didn't, then they wouldn't be around! *HMM...* I wonder if Justine gets along with her little sister.

And, just like that, I'm back in the story.

March 22nd

(I think it's someone's birthday today, but I can't remember who. Not important.) I know it's irrelevant, but the weather is getting nicer. Spring is finally around the corner!

We had exams when we came back from spring break.

DOWNER.

We've got the three musketeers together, and we are trying to figure out what to do with our **exclusive club**. I looked on the web to try to find out what's so cool about them, but there's nothing out of the ordinary. Except...

THERE ARE 4 OF THEM?!?

The Three Musketeers is a novel written by Alexandre Dumas in 1844. They were called: **D'Artagnan, Athos, Porthos and Aramis**. By definition, a musketeer is a **foot soldier**** (??) armed with a **musket**** (??)

I can't even find the dictionary. Unless... it's in Melia's room? *HMM...* That's a good excuse to poke through her room. I should actually go in and try to find it. And **TOO BAD** if I happen to find her *DIARY*!

ANYWAY... The musketeers fought for king **Louis XIII** (the name rings a bell, so I assume he was important). It's not a big deal, but we call our club

The Three Musketeers

Hmm... should we get a logo??

<u>After thinking for a few minutes...</u>

Should we ask Tommy** to be our fourth musketeer? *OMG,* this is confusing (**not Tommy). We should have been the **Three Wise Men** **(not the Three Stooges, ha ha)**. There were really three of them.

I have an idea: we'll form our country with the Three Musketeers!!!

P.S. ** I need to speak to Joje. He could become our 4th musketeer. But first, I would need to introduce him to my friends, because they don't know each other.

P.P.S. ** He always has to have a say in everything, not sure this is the best idea.

I'll talk to the others first.

April 1st
(The school should have been closed today.)

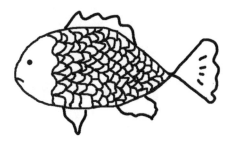

I wanted to play an April's Fool joke on William, but couldn't think of one. We had a major SNOW STORM last night. NIGHTMARE! We're all sick of the snow. But that's typical, around here. Snow at any time, just when you don't expect it! And to think we didn't get snow before DECEMBER 29 this year

(uh, I mean **LAST YEAR**, because it was before January 1ˢᵗ).
I would prefer if it snowed earlier in the year
(November) and was over by the end of March.

What I don't get is that *WIARTON WILLIE*
(the groundhog from Ontario) didn't see its shadow on
FEBRUARY 2ᴺᴰ this year. Spring should already
be here.

The American one, ~~Pung Punsx Panxung Punxang~~?,
UH, something **Phil** didn't either. So I guess they are
BOTH WRONG. We can't trust them anymore.

I prefer the Ontario groundhog. Its name is much less complicated
to pronounce. Seriously, ~~Puns Punxaw Pant Punt Puntua Punxsat-uw Punxasntuney~~

PUNXSUTAWNEY!!

I CAN'T WRITE IT WITHOUT LOOKING IT UP!!

It's even harder to pronounce.
Here's how it should be:

ponk-so-tâ-ny

or something like it...

I walk in the kitchen, mom is preparing
dinner.

Er, we're really having a BBQ??? My dad loves barbecuing, and we eat it *365 DAYS* a year, but, really, with two feet of snow outside?

Me: I can't remember, is it good or bad when the groundhog doesn't see its shadow?
Mom: Um, that's a very good question. I always forget.
Me: For real??
Mom: Yes.
Me: What do you mean, you don't know?
Mom: Well... I don't know everything!
Me: Er... YES you do!

Mom laughs out loud.

Mom: Which is it? I'm curious.
Me: Well, I'm asking myself the same thing, because I don't know!

Mom: Look it up on the web.
Me: Don't feel like it.
Mom: Really? That's a first! You love being on your iPad!

BULL'S EYE!!! I hate it when she's right.

Me: Yeah, but to play! Not to learn! I keep that for school.
Mom: Look it up and tell me, please. I'm not at school, anymore. How should I know?

I CAN SEE THAT SHE'S MOCKING ME.

Me (sarcastic): Ha. Ha. Very funny.
Mom: All I know, is that there are groundhogs everywhere now. Dunkirk Dave, Buckeye Chuck... Sir Walter Wally....
Me: What!? What's the point of having all those groundhogs?
Mom: No idea! But I'll bet they all make good money with those groundhogs.
Me: How can they tell if the groundhog sees its shadow or not? I mean, they can't ask, right??
Mom: Excellent point! I've been asking myself the same question for forty years!

Er... forty-four, but, hey, who's counting... She's in a good mood today. Bad timing to remind her of her **"real" age**. ;-)

Shadow or not, if my calculations are right, February 2nd was *EIGHT WEEKS AGO!* **(two months!)** It should be spring!

P.S. ** From now on, to hell with the groundhogs, **MOTHER NATURE** is the only one who decides!!

April 4th

(In my room, sitting on the floor, my back against the bed – not very comfortable, but it's different.)

We're going to my grand-parents' for Easter. Max is staying in Montreal, and we all wanted to go to William's cottage, once again, but my mom refused categorically. (She walks into my room... without knocking.)

Mom: Invite William along!
Me: Er, no way!

Mom: Why not?

Because I have the worst family in the world and he won't want to be my friend anymore?

OH CRAP! There she goes again with her boring and irrelevant theories... **blah blah blah.** She goes on, for the hundredth time about how Easter is a family Holiday, and we should celebrate together **blah blah blah.**

My point is that Easter is during a **long week-end** and celebrating on Sunday ruins the whole weekend **(because we have Monday and Friday off)** I say we should celebrate on Monday night, so we can have the whole weekend to do what we want, with our friends, not our family.

Me: Okay, I'll ask William.

<u>I already know the answer:</u>
"Yesssssss!!!!!" or "AWESOME!!"

Mom leaves my room.

**(This is irrelevant, but I stand to sit at my desk because my bum is numb).

So confused, right now.

Going to church on **Sunday** breaks up the weekend, and I'm mad at my parents for **FORCING ME TO GO.** Not that I don't like it... but I don't like it.

I must say though, the priest at my church is the most hilarious one ever!!! He rrrrrrrrrrrrrrrrrrrrrrrrolls his "**RRRRRRRRRS**" and he's no less than *204 YEARS-OLD*... **before Christ!!!**

P.S. ** All right, he's not THAT old, but he's at least 75 years old... or 90...

P.P.S. ** While I'm there, I might as well thank God for what I have. I am spoiled (or so my parents say) and my family loves me (even if half of it gets on my nerves).
But I'll keep this to myself.

You better.

April 7th
At my grandparents'.

My grandma is the best cook in the WORLD!

I LOOOOOOVE visiting my grandparents!! William was alone – well with his nanny, but she doesn't count (**his parents are gone I don't know where, but I know it's an island in the Atlantic... er, no, the Pacific Ocean? Anyway, it's the ocean with the bigger waves), so he came with us. He enjoys going to mass. He was praying hard, I tell you. I wonder what he asked for.

HE ALREADY HAS EVERYTHING.

I prayed for:
- New skis
- A new tennis racket
- A new big sister
- Skates
- Everything I don't have

P.S. ** William finally met Joje. But not at church, because he didn't go. They met us directly at my grandparents'. His parents are cooler than mine. **lucky him.

Grandma made a typical **Easter meal**. Her ham is so good, I always ask for seconds *OH*, and **two portions of dessert**, especially pieces of her famous **sugar pie**! She also made a maple pie... and an awesome caramel pudding. Needless to say William jumped on it!!**

** ER, SO TO SPEAK...

I had so much sugar that I was **buzzed** all afternoon!

Melia spent the whole day on FaceTime with **Simon**, even if they saw each other last night. When the weather was nice, she sat on the porch and sunbathed for a **few hours**. Her skin's going to **WRINKLE** prematurely (= and she will look like a raisin at age 40). She doesn't put sunscreen on because she says she tans faster without it.

I played with the **Twins**, Joje, Joje's little ~~annoying~~ brother, and William. The twins love it when we **PLAY TOGETHER**, and we needed more players for our game, so it turned out perfect!

** Wouldn't it be cool to bump into **Justine**?

<u>Thinking to myself...</u>

**WHAT???

It could happen! It's a small world, isn't it?

April 8ᵗʰ

Home = I played video games all day (☺), because the weather sucks. (☹)

**No sign of Justine today.

P.S. ****Seriously**... I wonder what William asked "God" in church.

To: willywonka16@(secret!!).com
From: Charlie4428@(secret!!).com
Hey William, what's up?

To: Charlie4428@(secret!!).com
From: willywonka16@(secret!!).com
Nothing much. Just watching TV with the nanny.

P.S. **I must figure out a way to find out what William asked for.

To: willywonka16@(secret!!).com
From: Charlie4428@(secret!!).com
Hmm... Curious to know if my prayers will be answered.

To: Charlie4428@(secret!!).com
From: willywonka16@(secret!!).com
What prayers?

To: willywonka16@(secret!!).com
From: Charlie4428@(secret!!).com
Well... you know... in church, the other day? I want to know what I'll get... What did you ask for?

To: Charlie4428@(secret!!).com
From: willywonka16@(secret!!).com
What do you mean?

To: willywonka16@(secret!!).com
From: Charlie4428@(secret!!).com
You have everything. What do you ask God for when you pray?

To: Charlie4428@(secret!!).com
From: willywonka16@(secret!!).com
Always the same... but I never get it.

I can understand. He's too young for a *FERRARI*.

To: willywonka16@(secret!!).com
From: Charlie4428@(secret!!).com

*(I can't help it.)

What?

To: Charlie4428@(secret!!).com
From: willywonka16@(secret!!).com
A family like yours.

P.S. ** My cheeks flush and I
suddenly feel bad while reading his
message, so I answer.

To: willywonka16@(secret!!).com
From: Charlie4428@(secret!!).com
Er, anyway, I never get what I want either. Don't
worry about it. Church is very confusing. When do
we need to stand up?? Anyway, talk to you later. Bye.

Sometimes, I should just know when to keep my
mouth shut.

April 9th

My room / the kitchen / Melia's room – ha ha / the basement.

**Didn't see Justine.
**irrelevant.

P.S. ** I stayed in the house and
played board games with the family.
It's pouring rain outside.

Melia was on FaceTime for half the day, and went shopping the other half. "Teenagers... they're not easy," mom always says.

April 10th

Worked on the lawn with dad and the twins...

*Still no sign of Justine.

April 11th

Errands = Costco + gas station for... gas (!!) + supermarket + (because I'm a good kid) coffee for Dad + a chocolate frappucino for me!!!

Because we've stayed in the house over the last few days, dad makes me run errands with him.

BUMMER

**except for the frappucino ☺

We walk into the **hardware store**.

I <u>hate</u> hardware stores.

We're walking up and down the aisles to find a small piece of ~~rubbish rubber~~ rubber for the toilet. No idea what it's for even if dad explained it to me a *HUNDRED TIMES*.

Me: Ask someone.
Dad: NO. I know what I want.
Me: What's it called?
Dad: I don't know, but it's small, round, and made of rubber, and it goes into the--
Me: Daaaad! You told me a million times! I don't know what it is! Ask someone!

I'm going to make a scene if he insists on not asking. We turn around the corner to walk up the next aisle and then I see her!! *NO WAY!?!* Can it really be her??

JUSTIIIIIIINE

OMG! I can't walk up to her, I'm way too shy –

Dad: Martin?!?

Er. Justine's dad turns around and walks up to us. Justine sees me. Breathe, Charles, her dress is not that nice. (What's that ~~beautiful~~ color called again?)

Martin: Wow!! How long has it been? Ten years?

They shake hands and start a conversation.

blah blah blah.

Justine (To me): Hi.
Me: Hi.

Okay, this is AWKWARD. I have, like, **nothing** to say to her.

Justine: Did you start the French project?

Me (being as cool as usual): Pff... Of course.

Er... I'm not lying. I did open the book the other day, and I was planning on opening it again... soon.

Justine: Cool.

Hmm... She seems shy. Is that possible?
(Our dads = blah blah blah)

Me: You're running errands with your dad?

I'm officially an idiot.

Justine: No.
Me: N-no?
Justine: Of course!! What do you think I'm doing? Laundry??
Me: Er...

... Just trying to make conversation to break the ice, in case you didn't notice.

Me: Sorry, I'm an idiot when I'm shy.

That's it!! She bursts out laughing! *PHEW!!*

MOM'S RIGHT: THERE'S NOTHING LIKE TELLING THE TRUTH!!

**Sometimes. But not always...

So we start talking about things and we are both finally comfortable.

> **She thinks it's pretty *COOL* that I am friends with William now and she smiled when I told her about the Three Musketeers... We just need to find a purpose.

Maybe we should learn fencing?

I should try it. I'm sure I would be above average.

P.S. ** But I also need to discuss the "new country" idea with the boys.

Hmm... I have a smile on my face all night.

April 12th

Nothing special ... in my room **(didn't think about Justine that much)**.

Oh. There's another lie. She's all I have been thinking about in the last few hours.

At night

(FaceTime with Joje, at *19 H 47*)

Joje: My mom said I could invite you over for the weekend. Do you feel like it?
Me: When?
Joje: I don't know! When you're free!
Me: I'll ask my mom and get back to you, okay?

P.S. ** I'll ask her tomorrow night, because I should already be in bed tonight...

April 13th

Uh-oh, I'm grounded in my room because I tossed a pink bra of my sister's out in front of her friends today.

Mom is raging.

No sense of humour **in this family**.

The door opens. My mom + dad walk in = that can't be good. Mom was probably waiting for dad to get home before coming in... So they can punish me together.

Mom: Charlie, Dad and I would like to talk to you (= hmm, this doesn't look like a "bra" conversation).
Dad: ...

P.S. ** In these situations, my dad never says a word. Can't blame him, my mom has a lot to say, and she's got quite a temper when she's mad. I would stay quiet, too, if I were him...

Me (I think I know what they want to talk about): What is it?
Mom: Do you know?
Me (I shrug, but she's a witch, so she probably knows I know...): ...
Dad: ...
Mom: It's regarding your grades.
Me: ...
Dad: ... (He's staring at me, probably waiting for mom to go on... like me)
Mom: I got a call from Miss Howard.

Me: No way?!?

There goes my chances of going to my cousin's house...

P.P.S. ** I need to find a good excuse to tell Joje. I'll tell him I need to help dad with... something, so I can't go to his house. I won't even bother to ask mom if I can go, I already know the answer.

Mom: She tells me you have been neglecting your studies, and that you didn't do well in your exams.
Me: ...
Dad: ... **

** (he's worthless, right now, and it's really annoying.)

178

Mom: Why didn't you tell us before?

Uh... because I didn't ~~care~~ know.

Me: (I shrug).
Dad: ...
Mom: From now on, I want to see your report card and your planner every day.
Me: What!?! Noooooo!! Come on!!
Dad: ... * *

** HE BETTER SAY SOMETHING OR I'M GOING TO LOSE IT!

Mom: Come on! You're 11 and you act like Tutu!!!
If I need to study with you, I'll do it! But you're going
to raise your grades. Understood?
Me: ...
Dad:

P.S. ** If he doesn't say anything in the
next 10, uh, 30 seconds I swear, I don't know
what I'm going to do.

Mom: You're lucky I have time to help you. You
wouldn't like summer school.
Dad: Mom's right.

P.S. ** It's about time...

Mom: Look at me when I'm talking to you.
Me: Yeah yeah.

Mom: And watch how you speak to me, because you're really not in a position to act this way.

** She's a witch, she scares me, I will obey.

Me: Okay.

Mom: Oh. I took the liberty of asking Miss Howard how Max and William are doing in class. She says William is top of the class... And Max is doing really well.

WHAT? William is top of my class? He never told me that!?!

That's embarrassing.

Evening

(It's *18 H 07*, right before dinner... another family dinner that is)

To: max3875@(secret!!)
From: Charlie4428@(secret!!)
Did you know William was top of our class?

To: Charlie4428@(secret!!)
From: max3875@(secret!!)
No, but I know he always scores really high.
He had 94% in the essay, and 99% in dictation.

To: max3875@(secret!!)
From: Charlie4428@(secret!!)
REALLY??? How is it possible to get 94% in
writing?? I never scored more than... uh, well...
and... my stories are good,... I think.

To: Charlie4428@(secret!!)
From: max3875@(secret!!)
Tell me about it. I never had more than 83%.
And in dictation, no more than 89%.

I'VE NEVER HAD A MARK OVER 71%.

To: max3875@(secret!!)
From: Charlie4428@(secret!!)
I hear you... Got to go. See you tomorrow.

The witch is right. I need to study and get those
grades up. I feel like a loser. It's really not cool to
get bad grades, especially if my friends have good ones.
I don't want to be the reject of the THREE MUSKETEERS
(I'm really the coolest one!).

Okay, so where's that English book?

182

April 21st

Sitting at my desk, nose in my books... **NO JOKE**:
- no music;
- no FaceTime;
- no snack *only a glass of water;
- ~~no distractions, like thinking about Justine.~~

I've been studying for a week (= a lot = tremendously), and I got my dictation grade... *87%.*

Never had that MY WHOLE LIFE!!

Me: MOO-OOOMM!!!

This is a great time to show mom. William invited Max and me to his cottage on the weekend of the 7TH. She sooooo has to say yes.

<u>A few minutes later</u> – after showing her my grade.

Mom: You see, when you want to, you can... It's not witchcraft...

> IN MY HEAD = uh... certainly not for you, you're a witch.

Me: You're right.

P.S. **I should really tell her she's right if I want her on my side.

Me (hesitating): Mom?
Mom: Yes, honey?
Me (She's going to say no, she's going to say no, she's going to say no. I should wait for my math marks. **I'll have more leverage with TWO good grades. She won't have a choice but to say yes): Uh, ... What's for dinner?
Mom: What do you really want to ask me?

P.S. **Supernatural powers confirmed.

He he...

Me: Uh, n-nothing, I swear (fingers crossed behind my back) just want to know what we're eating tonight.

P.S. **I can see in her eyes that she doesn't believe me.

Mom: Lemon veal scallops with noodles.

**My favourite!

Mom: It'll be ready in a few minutes.
Me: Cool...
Mom: Anything else you want to ask?

I just can't ask right now, so I shake my head "no".

P.S. ****She doesn't believe me **AT ALL**.
It's so obvious.

Mom: Okay then.

I need to score high in my maths test. I'll cross my fingers until I get my grade. PLEAAAAAAASE God. I'll do whatever needs to be done.

PLEAAAAAAAAAAAAAAAAAAAAAAAASE!

*But I won't apologize to Melia.

FaceTime that evening

It's 8:16pm... Yeah yeah, turning the lights off in a few!

Joje: So?
Me: Not sure... I may need to study.
Joje: Oh... What if I tell her I'll study with you?
Me: Like she's going to believe you!! No way!! Ask your mom to call mine. Maybe she can convince her.
Joje: No way!! My mom's afraid of yours!!

P.S. ****Can't blame her.

Me: William also invited me to to his cottage and I don't think I can go.

April 23rd

Doesn't matter where I am... Okay, I'm upstairs in the hallway. WHAT?? I'm not grounded, might as well enjoy it.

DIDN'T GET MY GRADE FOR MATHS, YET. ☹

April 24th

Who cares? I'm grounded but I won't say why because I'm too frustrated right now. But Melia will pay for it this time.

STILL NO GRADE. ☹

April 25th

Miss Howard walks up to my desk and hands me my math exam. I close my eyes, incapable of looking at her. My future is at stake here. If I flunk, I –

Miss Howard: Well done, Charles!

What? Did she just congratulate me? I open one eye to see how I did.

79% Yippee!!!
*I'm so NOT mad anymore!

<u>As soon as I walk in the house...</u>
(We carpooled today with a friend of my mom's...)

Me: MOO-OOOMM!!!

Mom (dry tone): What is it?
Me (she doesn't look happy. No good mood here): Uh...
You don't look so happy?
Mom: I'm not. I had a day from he– **(she corrects herself)** a very bad day. And I have a migraine. And I have to prepare dinner. What is it? Make it quick.
Me: Uh... I got 79% on my math exam.
Mom: Good. Knew you could do it.

> Uh... What about? = Way to
> go Charles! Wow! Super! I'm
> sooooo proud!

GOOD??

*P.S. *** She's not enthusiastic at all. And she's holding her head. *TIME TO ABORT MY MISSION!* I'll ask her when she gets better, other wise I know she'll say **NO.**

187

She leaves the kitchen for a nap in the living room.

CRAP!

To: Charlie4428@(secret!!)
From: willywonka16@(secret!!)
And?? Did she say yes!??

To: willywonka16@(secret!!)
From: Charlie4428@(secret!!)
Er... She's not home tonight, I'll ask her tomorrow.

To: Charlie4428@(secret!!)
From: willywonka16@(secret!!)
That sucks! Max just wrote me and he's coming.

AAARGH! WHY IS MY MOTHER SO... AAARGH!?

AREN'T MY GRADES BETTER???

April 27th

Near the lockers, in the hallway.

William: Hi.
Me: Hi.
William: So? Can you come?
Me: Er... Didn't see her, she wasn't home.
William: Still out? I thought she never went out?
Me: Well, uh... She's got a busy week at the office, that's why.
William: You don't see her in the morning?
Me: No, she... sleeps in.

AWKWARDNESS (=LONG AWKWARD SILENCE)

I hate lying to my friends.

Evening
About 7:17pm

Me (To myself): Okay. I have to ask her tonight, or else the boys will think I'm a douchebag.

P.S. ** I'll be a bigger one if my mom says no.

We should get our writing grades tomorrow. I should ask her tonight, just in case... I don't feel super confident about my grade... I mean, it's not really my fault. The subject we had to work on really sucked.

Me: Moooo-ooom!?!

Dad (Walking in my room): What's up?
Me: Dad? Where's mom?
Dad: She just left! Didn't you hear her saying good night??
Me (crap!): Oh... No, I didn't hear her.
Dad: No worries. What do you need?

My dad's usually cool about these things, he never says NO. He's like, incapable of saying no. I should have asked him from the start. I don't know why I didn't think about it...

Me: William invited Max and me to spend the weekend at his cottage up north. Can I go?
Dad (without hesitation?!?): No.
Me: What do you mean, NO?

P.S. ** He NEVER says NO!! What's his problem tonight??

Dad: Your grandparents will be back from their trip and we're going to see them.
Me: AGAIN?? But we saw them at Easter!!
Dad: Yes, and last Christmas, and the one before, right?!! Really, Charlie, they're your grandparents, consider yourself lucky to be able to see them so often.
Me: Could I go the week after?
Dad: I don't think so. Let me discuss it with mom tomorrow.

I'm screwed. There's no way she'll agree to this.

She always says *NO*. It's impossible for her to say "yes". It's not in her nature. She's just incapable. Sucks **BIG TIME**.

** (Doorbell.)

Dad: Ah! That's the pizza!! Let's go!!

He leaves my room **as if nothing happened!!** I'm not hungry anymore. **(5 second pause)** I looove pizza. I'll make an effort.

[On my way down to the kitchen = I'm thinking to myself]

When did dad learn to say "*NO*"?? As a man, shouldn't he understand what it means to me??? Hmm...
I can't wait to form my own country...
(I'll ask my mother tomorrow anyway.)

FaceTime
(It's *20 H 38* = I get to go to bed later when my mom's not around – **ha ha!**)

Joje: Did you find a name for our country?
Me: Not yet. Everything is already taken.
Joje: I know, it's crazy.

(Rolling my eyes, right now)

8:47PM...

To: Charlie4428@(secret!!)
From: willywonka16@(secret!!)

So?

To: willywonka16@(secret!!)
From: Charlie4428@(secret!!)
Uh... you won't believe me, but, er... we have guests over for dinner tonight. I didn't know... They're, um, friends of my grandparents, and they're in town only today.

To: Charlie4428@(secret!!)
From: willywonka16@(secret!!)
Come on! Ask her anyway!!

To: willywonka16@(secret!!)
From: Charlie4428@(secret!!)
Impossible. They're really annoying and my mom's stressed out like crazy... I'd rather not get in her way tonight.

To: Charlie4428@(secret!!)
From: willywonka16@(secret!!)
Ask her after dinner, when they're gone.

To: willywonka16@(secret!!)
From: Charlie4428@(secret!!)
Uh, impossible... er, to be nice, my dad invited them over for the night. They're sleeping here. I'm so frustrated.

To: Charlie4428@(secret!!)
From: willywonka16@(secret!!)
Okay then, let's wait until tomorrow... That sucks big time...

UH OH. William is disappointed...

8:58PM BUSY NIGHT...

From: max3875@(secret!!)
To: Charlie4428@(secret!!)
What the heck???? I don't believe the "guests" story. Friends of your grandparents??? Come on!

From: Charlie4428@(secret!!).com
To: max3875@(secret!!).com
What?!? You don't believe me?? I am insulted that you'd even suggest I could be lying!

From: max3875@(secret!!).com
To: Charlie4428@(secret!!).com
I know you, Charlie, you're always too shy to ask your mom anything. I know what's going to happen:

You're going to ask her at the last minute, and she'll say no, and you're going to be mad. Can you just stop acting like a baby and ask her already?

(To myself= Uh?!? A baby??)

Or else I'm calling your house and asking her myself.

Get it????

From: Charlie4428@(secret!!)
To: max3875@(secret!!)
Whoa! Don't get over excited! My mom's out tonight. I asked my father but he said "no". So I'll ask my mom tomorrow.

From: max3875@(secret!!)
To: Charlie4428@(secret!!)
What?!? Your dad said "NO"??? That's impossible?? He never says "NO". Okay, I believe you Charlie. But ask your mom tomorrow. I just hope she's distracted and she agrees...

From: Charlie4428@(secret!!)
To: max3875@(secret!!)

YOU TELL ME. I'm going to pray all night...

Please don't tell William I was lying. I feel like such a jerk as it is. You know how my mom is, I need to find the right timing with her.

From: max3875@(secret!!).com
To: Charlie4428@(secret!!).com
It's almost unbelievable that your dad refused. It's like everything is upside down!

From: Charlie4428@(secret!!).com
To: max3875@(secret!!).com
He must have fallen on his head. I'll ask her
tomorrow. Will we get our writing grade tomorrow?

From: max3875@(secret!!).com
To: Charlie4428@(secret!!).com
I don't know. Who cares? What's important is our
boys' weekend! Come on, Charles, you're like
d'Artagnan!!! You must convince her!!

From: Charlie4428@(secret!!).com
To: max3875@(secret!!).com
D'Artagnan? I thought we weren't changing our
names? That it was too complicated?? And, didn't
you want to be D'Artagnan? I'm confused. Anyway,
I'm going to bed. I'll see you tomorrow.

11:26pm
I'm in bed (but incapable of sleeping because I'm thinking about
my always-negative-mother).

She **HAS** to say "yes". Please, pleaaaaaaaaase, say *YES*.

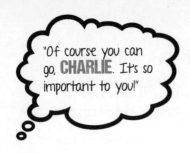

"Of course you can go, **CHARLIE**. It's so important to you!"

April 28th

Stalling in the hallway, thinking about how to ask her. When I feel an ounce of courage entering my body, I walk into the kitchen.

*I FEEL MOTIVATED WHEN I WALK INTO THE KITCHEN...

Me: Hmmmmmm... It smells awesome!

P.S. **She looks at me like she doesn't believe me. Maybe I overplayed it? She freaks me out.

She's cutting veggies... I have a piece, to stall.
**(I grab a carrot, even if I prefer celery. I know she'll notice *MY EFFORT*.)

Me: Mmm...
Mom: You never say that while eating carrots. What's going on?
Me: Nothing.

She's staring. Oh, oh... That's it! I'm in trouble. She knows I'm lying... you know... a witch would know...

P.S. ** This silence is eternal. I have to say something.

Me: Uh... Grandma and grandpa are coming back on Saturday?
Mom: Yes. You must be excited to see them, right? To hear about their trip?

{ ** I can't remember where they were... India? Not sure... Who cares... }

Me: Yeah...

(= NO, but it's important to stay polite when I talk about my grandparents.)

Long endless pause that seems like two weeks...

Mom: You don't sound convinced.
Me: Uh... (Now or never. Common, Charles, you can do it!) It's just that, well... I am, but William had invited Max and me to his cottage for the weekend, and it would have been nice for the three of us to be together for a couple of days. I would've really liked to go, but I understand that seeing my grandparents is also important.

I spoke very slowly, and calmly, to make sure mom understands my disappointment. You know??

Mom: Bah, I'm sure they'll understand.
Me: I know, but William really wanted me to go.
Mom: Oh, I know. I'm talking about my mom and dad...

She winks at me. Does that mean "yes"?? She likes to play tricks on me, so I don't want to get excited too quickly, but my heart is racing.

BOOM BOOM BOOM BOOM

Me: You're kidding, right?
Mom: Unless you don't want to go?
Me: Are you crazy?!? I'm DYING to go!!
I lean to kiss her (she deserves it!), but...

Mom: What did you get in your essay?

She asked with a huge smile on her face. DARN! I know it was a trap. She's NEVER this nice.

Me: Uh...

It's so mean of her to play with my emotions like this. She should've asked BEFORE letting me go! AARGH I should've done better. But I HATE essays. My grades are NEVER good!

Mom: Uh... How much?
Me: You're going to be mad.

{ OH, OH, BYE BYE SMILEY FACE... }

Mom: How much?
Me: ... **(I show her: 73%.)**

Mom: *73%?* Wow! Isn't this your best score since the beginning of the year?

I can suddenly breathe again.

Me: Yeah, but I could have done better.
Mom: It's gone up! Don't only focus on the grade, Charlie, look at your improvement!! You're usually between 58 and 70.

ME = UH, BETWEEN 58 AND 71!

Mom: 73%, is good. Keep up the good work, I'm very proud of you!

She leaves the kitchen. I'm confused, she's so weird. **Incomprehensible**. But, then again, dad always says: "The fact that I married her doesn't mean I understand everything she says/does."

YIPPPEEEE!!!!

To: willywonka16@(secret!!).com
Cc: max3875@(secret!!).com
From: Charlie4428@(secret!!).com
Hey guys!
Guess what? My mom said "YES"!!!!!
YESSSSSSSS!!!!
The Three Musketeers reunited for the weekend!!!!

6:12pm

When I go up to my room after dinner, I check my emails. No news from the boys.
I wait *15 MINUTES*.

7:25pm

Still no news *(!?!?!?!)*. I grab the phone.

Max: Hello?
Me: Hey Max
Max: Hey Charlie.
Me: So, my mom wants me to go to William's this weekend.
Max: Cool. Listen, can we talk tomorrow? I'm in the middle of something.

(CLICK) = HE HUNG UP.

COOL?!?

I thought he'd be happier than "cool". I would have said: YEAH!!! SUPER COOOOLL!!!!! **Or:** Can't wait!!!

Or else: Your mom's finally coool!! I can't believe it!! It's going to be the best weekend EVER!!

Yeah! I think it's pretty cool!

I'm calling William. I know he'll react better.

NOT LIKE MAX.

William (like, with his mouth full): HELLO?
Me: Hi. How's it going?
William (his mouth is still full?): Hmm...

DOESN'T HE EVER SWALLOW????

Me: Did you read my email?
William: Yeah. Cool.
Me: Yeah, I'm really happy. I was thinking, maybe we should----
William (He interrupts me!): Charlie, let's talk tomorrow. Okay?
Me: Okay.
William: Ciao!

(CLICK) = HE HUNG UP.

SINCE WHEN IS HE TOO BUSY TO TALK? HE'S ALWAYS BY HIMSELF AND HE NEVER DOES ANYTHING IN THE EVENINGS!?!

This is really not the reaction I was expecting. Maybe I interrupted his dinner?

** by that, I mean a boring dinner with his boring nanny who doesn't speak his language??

We'll see tomorrow.
I go to bed a little (a lot) disappointed... but so happy to be going! ☺

Okay, let's start counting... Quick!

April 28th
Near the lockers, in the school basement.

Max is searching for something in his locker. I walk up to him.

Me: What is it? You're not happy I'm going to William's?
Max: Why do you say that?
Me: When I called, last night...
Max: I was being grounded by my mother...

Me: Why?
Max: I didn't do well in my essay. Worse grade of the year.
Me: How much?
Max: 74%.

[OUCH]

Me: Ohhh...
Max: Don't mention it. I feel like such a loser. Hey, promise you won't tell anyone?
Me: No. No worries.
Max: But you must have scored high if your mom's letting you go, right?
Me: Uh...

** WILLIAM WALKS UP TO US AT THIS MOMENT (MY SAVIOR).

Me: Hey, William, what were you doing when I called you last night?

William: Nothing much, why?
Me: Well, uh... Nothing. No reason.

(Long pause)

**But it bothers me...

Me: You were doing nothing? like, **really** nothing?
William: Don't think so. Can't remember.
Me: Aaah...(I change the subject) We should make an itinerary.
Max: Itinerary?
Me: I mean, you know, a list of things to do.
Max: Like an agenda?
Me: Yeah, that's it! I'll do it tonight and send it to you guys, okay?
William: Oooh, Justine's coming this way.
Max: Come on, Will. (To me) We'll leave you alone!

They like to tease me with JUSTINE... I don't mind it. It's cool. They **leave us**.

Justine (walks up to me): Hi Charlie!
Me: Hey Justine! Hadn't seen you!

P.S. ** Excellent liar.

Justine: How's it going?
Me: Good, you?
Justine: Great...
Me: ...
Justine: ...
Me: ...

Justine: So, you're going to William's this weekend?
Me: Who told you?
Justine: My sister. Your sister told her.
Me: Huh?... Yeah, Max and I. Should be fun...
Justine: Cool...
Me: Cool.

Me: Oh! We should go!
Justine: Want to walk with me?
Me: Okay.

OH OH. Hopefully, Lulu didn't say anything too compromising to Charlotte. It's in her **DNA**. She's the queen of ruining everything **(especially my life)**.

1:08 PM – 2:08 PM – 2:38 PM – 2:48 PM – 3:08 PM – 3:28 PM

That's weird. There's always an *8*. It's that kind of day I guess...

Maybe I'm a future witch or magician?

Long story short: I was tapping my foot all afternoon...

P.S. ******I wonder what Lulu and Charlotte talk about...

AFTER SCHOOL...

*When school is over, at 3:35 pm.

P.P.S. ******What do Charlotte and Lulu talk about when they talk about us?

Lulu: Nothing much.
Me: Nothing much like what, let's say?
Lulu: Justine likes you too!!!
Me: WHAT??????? Why do you say that?
Lulu: Because Charlotte told me.
Me: Why did she tell you?
Lulu: Because I told her you had a crush on Justine.
Me: **WHAT?????????**

Mom shows up... Bad timing.

(Lulu is proud, but I'm freaking out, and I'm sweating all over... even in places I didn't know could sweat. NO JOKE.)

Once home, I go directly to Lulu's room.

Me: Tell me you were kidding, that you never said that!!

206

Lulu: Why? I wanted to help you!

Me: Help me?!? You can help me by minding your own business!!!

Lulu (looks at me for a brief moment. Her eyes get wet): MOOOOO-OOOOOOM!!!

Me: Argh, never mind. It's okay.

No time to be grounded: my mom would be happy to forbid me to go to William's.

Me: I'd like to keep it to myself, next time, okay?

Lulu: Sorry, I just wanted to be nice, because I know you're shy... You're my older brother, and I want you to be happy.

{ Uh... my happiness, really?!?
She's more "adult" than I am!?!? }

And she's so cute, I melt like a POPSICLE.

Me: Come here, my beautiful favourite little sister.

(Might as well butter it up.)

Aaawn...

I lean down to hold her in my arms, but she jumps on me.

Lulu: Charlie, you're the best big brother in the whole world!!!

She holds me so tight I am having a hard time breathing. She lets go of me and leaves my room. *PHEW...* Deep down, I'm kind of glad there's a possibility that Justine might have a crush on me too. It's probably why she came and talked to me today

COOL!

I sort of, kind of have a girlfriend *(???)*.

I sit and make a list... Uh, I mean, an agenda.

To: willywonka16@(secret!!).com
Cc: max3875@(secret!!).com
From: Charlie4428@(secret!!).com
Hey guys!
Here's a list of what we should do this weekend.
Let me know your thoughts.

THINGS TO DO AT WILLIAM'S:

- Listen to heavy metal music. Especially AC/DC, because they're soooo cool. **(Mom hates it when I listen to them – don't know why.)** I also like Metallica and Megadeth, but not all their songs... just a few. Like, really only a few.
- Eat popcorn with M&M's ** for William!
- Define the THREE MUSKETEERS Club.

*We need a name for our country.

- Watch PSYCHO and the AMITYVILLE (horror movies).
- Eat popcorn with M&M's again, for William... again!

A few minutes later...

To: Charlie4428@(secret!!).com
Cc: willywonka16@(secret!!).com
From: max3875@(secret!!).com

Okay. But could we watch the Harry Potter *movies instead? I have seen the first five, but I wouldn't mind seeing them again. And I love magic! We should do a sorcerer's club instead of the THREE MUSKETEERS, what do you think?*

To: Charlie4428@(secret!!).com
Cc: : max3875@(secret!!).com
From: willywonka16@(secret!!).com

I'm in. But how can we become real sorcerers? We don't know how to... And magic doesn't exist... You know that, right? Ha ha.

To: willywonka16@(secret!!).com
Cc: : max3875@(secret!!).com
From: Charlie4428@(secret!!).com

Don't mind him, Will, he is making fun of Tommy. We are not doing a sorcerer's club as fun as it may be. I think we will have our hands full with the Three Musketeers, no?

To: Charlie4428@(secret!!).com
Cc: : max3875@(secret!!).com
From: willywonka16@(secret!!).com

Let's decide this weekend. Oh... but Max, if you were not joking, I have all of the HP movies!! He he...

To: willywonka16@(secret!!).com
Cc: max3875@(secret!!).com
From: Charlie4428@(secret!!).com
I don't mind watching the movies, as long as we don't get obessesed over them. We have lots to accomplish this weekend!

To: Charlie4428@(secret!!).com
Cc: : willywonka16@(secret!!).com
From: max3875@(secret!!).com
You're right Charlie. Let's play it by ear!

To: Charlie4428@(secret!!).com
Cc: : max3875@(secret!!).com
From: willywonka16@(secret!!).com
Good idea, Max, let's do that!

To: willywonka16@(secret!!).com
Cc: max3875@(secret!!).com
From: Charlie4428@(secret!!).com
Alright. Bye.

We should definitely focus on the Three Musketeers Club. Don't want to lose more friends over Harry Potter.

I go to bed thinking about ~~Justine~~ William's cottage and all the fun things we are going to do!

Haven't been to the mountains in so long...

April 29th

School = boring. Even if Miss Howard is the coolest.

I don't know why, but it feels like today is longer than usual. Did someone turn the clock back a few hours??

I can't wait till tonight!

We're leaving for the cottage with William's mom. His dad's working, so he'll meet us there later on.

P.S. ** We stop for a bite on our way there. Soooo cool!! And I get to order whatever I want to, too. Even cooler!!!

Once we arrive, I take out the list I made of things to do. They say it's going to rain all day. Good! We'll get to play Ping-Pong and pinball. Hmm... We should have a tournament. *OH, AND WE'VE GOT TO DRINK HOT CHOCOLATE AND MARSHMALLOWS.* I love

William's cottage! We'll also watch movies, talk about our future country, and lots of other stuff!! There's so much to do, and so little time!!

April 30th

In the basement, where all the great stuff is (= pinball machine + popcorn maker + another pinball machine + an *Air Hockey table*). Mega storm outside + thunder + lightning = we have to stay inside (but I'm happy!).

I play on the pinball machine and it's great! (Oh! I just saw some major lightning.) I'm so good at it! I should become a professional pinball player. I'd break every world record! Let's say I play in tournaments and make *$1000* each time, I'll be rich after playing in only 20 tournaments (*=$20 000*).

$$$$$

There's a huge thunder clap and we all jump. **EVERYTHING SHUTS DOWN.** *CRAP!* I was about to beat my own record!!!

Me: Guys?
William: Oh no!?! Mooooom???
Voice of William's mom: It's alright, it's just an electricity outage. Are you guys okay?
Me: Ask her when we'll have power again.
William: Will it be long before it comes back on?

Voice of William's mom: No idea, honey.
Max: You don't have a generator?

A WHAT?!?

William: It's been broken for almost a year and my dad always forgets to have it repaired because we never use it. He doesn't think about it when he's not here.
Max: That sucks.
Me: He has no excuse now!

William turns to me and laughs.

William: We should talk about our THREE MUSKE-TEERS club.

I don't really feel like it. I'd rather keep playing. Can't he have someone over **NOW**? I mean, now would be the best time to take care of it, right?

$$\left\{ \text{No Pinball machine + No Hot chocolate + No popcorn + No TV = Nothing much to do...} \right\}$$

After an hour of arguing, here's what's been decided.

P.S. Won't write down the whole conversation because:
1) It would be too long
2) I don't remember it in detail.

THE THREE MUSKETEERS: We promise to

1) Tell each other everything. NO SECRETS. Even if we kiss a girl. **Not that I want to. Especially not Justine. (Not that I'm thinking about her.)**

2) Not tell our secrets to anyone else outside the club.

3) Help each other with homework (= **very good for me**).

4) Help anyone who's being bullied by Kevin.

5) Try to do activities together whenever we can.

6) Bring homemade sweets whenever we can (**a request from William**).

7) Ignore Melia when she talks to us.

8) TBD (**To be determined**)

9) TBD

10) Read **The Three Musketeers** by Alexandre Dumas. ***

> *** Because it's so long, we'll divide it in three. Each of us will read our part and then tell the others what happened in it. I took the middle part.

11) Plan a weekend of camping in the mountains this summer. (uh...in William's backyard.)

12) Repeat our mantra "One for all, and all for one" every time we're together. That's the Three Musketeers' rallying cry.

May 4th

(For all you Star Wars fans out there...)
Awesome weekend with the boys.

P.S. ** No time to write, too busy... playing.

It's crazy, we spent hours trying to find a name for our country and we just COULDN'T! It seemed so easy!

Had I known, I NEVER would have suggested we form our own country. Way too much trouble!!

**How did all the countries in the world find their name?!?

Back home from the country. The usual. Melia was whining because she broke up with Simon, AGAIN. And the twin leeches asked me 2000 QUESTIONS about what I did this weekend.

Lulu: But what did you do AFTER the pinball machine?
Me: Told you, there was a power outage.
Tutu: I don't believe you.
Me: What? Why?!?
Tutu: You're just saying that because you don't want to tell us what you did.
Me: Uh, no. It's true, ask William if you don't believe me.
Tutu: Okay. What's his number?
Me: Uh, you can't call him now he's at his aunt's with his parents.

Tutu stands firmly in front of me and crosses his arms. Straight face. I just want to laugh.

Tutu: You're lying.

Lulu imitates her twin.

Lulu: Yes. You're lying to us. His parents are never home.
Tutu: We don't believe you.

I don't either.

Here we go again. They will bug me until they hear what they want to hear.

Me: Okay, okay. (pause = for a dramatic effect)
After beating all my records on the pinball machine, we had hot chocolate with extra marshmallows, and we had popcorn with extra M&M's. Then, we had a pool tournament, a baby foot tournament, and a ping pong tournament. It was sick!! Best weekend EVER!!

The more I speak, the bigger the twins' eyes get.

GREAT! They'll leave me alone. I am too brilliant.

Lulu: Cool!!! Then what?
Me: What?
Lulu: What did you do after??
Me: Uh... nothing.
Tutu: I don't believe you.
Me: It was late! We went to bed!!
Tutu: You NEVER want to go to bed when mom tells you to!

Lulu speaks.

Lulu: Tutu is right.
Tutu: Common, tell us!
Lulu: Yes. We're not leaving your room until you tell us EVERYTHING.
Me: Are you dreaming, or what?

Two hours later, the twins are finally happy with my (almost) fake story. I'm beat, and I have to go to bed.

Me too.

The next morning...
In class, Justine walks up to me. ~~I love it when she comes up to talk to me.~~

Justine: Have you finished your oral presentation for Thursday?

Er??? Right... I think that rings a bell.

**Darn! Totally forgot.

Me: Uh, Of course!
Justine: What book did you chose?
Me: Uh... *The Three Musketeers*!
Justine: *The Three Musketeers*?
Me: Yes! Alexandre Dumas. You don't know it?
Justine: Of course I do! I read it three times!
Me: Cool...

{ Lucky her. I'll have to read it *FOR REAL*, *NOW*. I completely spaced out on that project. }

NERD.

May 7th
Comfy on the living room sofa.

Wow, the beginning of the novel is good!! A lot better than I thought! And I read fast. I'm at *PAGE 18* and I almost don't feel like skipping a page, even if it was written ages ago.

(D'Artagnan is not afraid of anything. I look like him).

218

Today, in the afternoon (at school). No clock, but I'd say it was about *12:30PM* because it was during lunch break ... in the bathroom.

I walk in the bathroom, and Kevin and his three stooges follow me in. *UH-OH.* I have a bad feeling about this, and I suddenly want to throw up. Unfortunately, there's only the five of us, and no one else. **I CAN'T LET THEM BULLY ME**. Anyway, if he does anything bad to me, he's going to be expelled from school. Not that it makes a difference at this present moment, but it gives me a little *COURAGE*.
I turn around...

Me: If you think you're scaring me, think again. And if you try anything, I'll--
Kevin: You'll what? Huh?? Why don't you try.
Idiot #1: Yeah, why don't you...

Uh, there are four of them... and, is it me or are they taller than usual?

> *P.S.* ** I'm shaking, but I can't let them know I'm scared.

Me: Don't make me...

Kevin turns around to his stooges and laughs out loud.

Kevin: Hoo hoo, I'm so scared!! **(His face gets serious and he's so close now I can smell his breath.)** Watch how you talk to me.

Me: There are people who laugh at the horse that would not dare to laugh at the master.

> ** *The Three Musketeers*, page 18.

He looks at me, clueless, like an IDIOT.

<u>Note to self</u>: <u>He is an idiot</u>. He doesn't know what I am talking about.

Me: I will not have him laugh when I laugh (Oooh... it's not written exactly like that, but Kevin wouldn't know the difference...) You're such a loser. Uh, and you don't scare me.

AT ALL.

P.S. ** (LIAR!!)
**Darn! I said « uh ».

He's still staring at me without saying a word. I am **D'ARTAGNAN**, and I am scared of no one. **EXCEPT MAYBE KEVIN**. But I stay *STILL*, my voice is firm, and I am about two inches from his nose. He seems uncomfortable (and I like it!).

OH BOY.

(My legs are going to fail me and my mouth is dry. I would like to leave and show him that he doesn't impress me, but my back is almost against the wall. I hope he doesn't jump me.)

P.S. *** But, like magic, William and Max appear in the bathroom.

William: Is there a problem, here?

P.S. *** When William crosses his arms, it's never good.

I turn to Kevin and his stooges.

Me: I'm not the one you should ask. **(To Kevin)** Is there a problem?* * *

*** OKAY, so I am bit more confident, now that William and Max are here. I feel like I just grew a **FEW INCHES!**

Kevin and his boys shake their heads **NO**. William hasn't moved a muscle, and he's standing firm. He's suddenly very imposing, and intimidating. **ESPECIALLY WITH HIS ARMS CROSSED IN FRONT OF HIM.**
I.... uh... I'm almost scared for Kevin.

William hates confrontations. And he hates fighting. So he says:

William: Let's go, guys. Let's go outside and enjoy the nice weather.

We leave!!!

*** Because I know no one will ever read this notebook, I'm allowing myself to write something I will NEVER tell anyone... NOT EVEN **THE MUSKETEERS**.

I was so scared I almost pe** in my pants. Thank goodness William got there when he did. I would have come out anyway, but boy am I glad I had backup! That's what the musketeers are for.

ALL FOR ONE, AND ONE FOR ALL!

After school...

In the car, driving back home. *3:44 PM*. This is what I call a BAD day. I was mad and said something I regret.

I told my mom she was a b****** (too ashamed to repeat it). I don't know what got into me, it just came out. I didn't even mean it. On the contrary, I have a super mom... uh... well... sometimes.

Oh boy

I am in my room and it's *3:52 PM, 3:53 PM, 3:54 PM, 3:55 PM, 3:56 PM, 3:57 PM.* Unfortunately, the time doesn't go by as fast as that reads.

Mom walks in.

I STIFFEN, because I am taken by surprise. I didn't expect her so soon. I know it was wrong, so I might as well apologize right away.

Me: I'm sorry.
Mom: Do you realize what you said to me?
Me: I know. I'm sorry. I didn't mean it.
Mom: You're staying in your room for the rest of the afternoon.

(I JUMP.)

Me: What?!?!?! But I'm supposed to play with Max in... (uh, I look at the clock) 18 minutes!!

P.S. Today is Friday.

Mom: You'll know better next time than to call me a b****. Not only is it insulting, it's bad language, and that's no way to talk to your mother.

She's right. I wasn't even mad at her. I was mad at Tutu.

Me: I apologized. Doesn't that count?
Mom: Of course it does!

PHEW. She understands. I apologized. Let's stop the drama. I'm most certainly not the first boy to call his mom a b****.

Me: ... (What's next? Isn't it her turn to speak?)

Silent pause. (I don't really feel like breaking it.) Is she keeping quiet on purpose? I said what I had to say.

I APOLOGIZED!

Mom: I'm sorry as well.

I frown, confused.

Me: Uh... Okay. Why?
Mom: For forbidding you to play with Max.

She stands up and leaves my room without saying a word. I am astounded / in shock / stunned / frozen like a block of ice. No time to react. She peeks her head back in.

Mom: By the way, I'm calling Max to let him know you won't be going. No phone and no computer for you until I say so.

Me: Aaaargh!! That's unfair!!

Mom: It was unfair to be called a b* * * * by my son!

AAAARGH!!! I see my leech brother Tutu peaking around the door frame *¢¢?%%$$. What about minding his own business??
HE GETS TO ME, BIG TIME.

SHE SLAMS THE DOOR!
**Was that really necessary??

I need a few seconds to recoup. Nothing much to do.
Except to write in my notebook! Or find a darn name

for **my country**. (Don't feel like reading *The Three Musketeers*, it's painfully borin–.) **AAARGH!** She's doing it on purpose so that Max will know I'm grounded. **UNFAIR.**

P.S. ** I hope my mom won't tell Max why I'm... grounded...

P.P.S. ** Of course she will. She loves it when I'm miserable or when I fail.

P.P.S. ** The good thing about this (**there is always a silver lining to everything**) is that it'll give me time to get up-to-date in my notebook!

I have an idea! I will tell them I got into a **"FIGHT"** with Melia. And if they don't know I'm grounded, I'll just tell them I had to help dad. Had to help him... uh, do... **what exactly?**

LET'S SEE:
- The twins painted me purple and I had to wash up. (__Impossible__: we don't have purple paint at home. **Blue?**)
- Melia broke my arm (__Impossible__: I'd have to wear a **fake cast** for a month).
- I had to cut down some trees? (__Impossible__: we don't have a **chainsaw** = phew!!).

I am not worried, it's always easy to make up stories with bratty twins in the house.

An hour and something later, there is a knock on my door.

Me (mad – but I could use some company)**:** Who is it?
Lulu: Lulu...

I notice the plate in her hands the second she opens the door... Cheese and crackers, to be precise. Oh, and a glass of water.

JUST LIKE A GUARD WOULD BRING HIS PRISONER IN ISOLATION.

Lulu: I brought you a snack.
Me: Did mom ask you?
Lulu: No, and don't tell her 'cause I don't want to get in trouble.

Okay, that's kind of nice. Can't complain there (even though I feel like a prisoner. Oh, wait! I **AM** a prisoner!).

Me: Thanks, my sweet Lulu. Come sit next to me.
Lulu (huge smile)**:** What were you doing?
Me: I was counting the cracks in my ceiling.
Lulu: ???
Me (I smile)**:** Kidding! It's a way of saying I was doing nothing.
Lulu: How's the Three Musketeers club doing?
Me: How do you know that?
Lulu: (she shrugs)
Me: Lulu?
Lulu: I sort of overheard you the other day when you were talking to William about it.

Me: You little rascal, you!

I mess up her hair and she giggles.

Lulu: Justine thinks it's pretty cool that you have a club.

My whole body **TIGHTENS**.

Me: What?!? You talked about it with her sister???
Lulu: Why shouldn't I?
Me: Luluuuuu!!! I thought I'd asked you not to talk about these things with Charlotte!!
Lulu: Sorry, I only meant well.

Of course, she did, and of course, I forgive her because she's just soooo charming.

**It's about time she gets older. She'll wear glasses, braces, and have pimples. It'll be easier to get mad at her. But I won't break her nose.

Me: If you keep talking like that, Justine will know everything about me!
Lulu: Is that wrong?
Me: Well... I don't know much about her.
Lulu: I do. That's why I'm here!

> Oh... My little sister, my ally?? I should name her our fourth musketeer. She doesn't look like it, but she could be quite the spy for ~~me~~ us.

But I'd rather have Joje as musketeer #4. **Could there be 5 of us?** *OH!* I have a better idea: I'll give her a "title" in my country. **

> ** Like "fake-minister of communications, or information. Isn't that what she'll be doing? Politicians do that in real life, give their friends great jobs, even if they don't have the right skills.

This way, she would feel important and feed me information about JUSTINE.

I slide closer to my sister.

Me: Er... really?
Lulu (nods proudly): Yes, sir! Justine has a diary and she writes a lot of stuff in it. She always mentions you, and how cute you are. She thinks you're funny, even if you farted in class once.

(I blush like a tomato, and my head's about to explode.)

I knew she had heard me. But now, it's confirmed, and she told **her sister**?? (Oh, and who else did she tell??)

Jeez...
I know who else! **All** of her friends. *OH*, They must laugh every time they see me.
I want to die.

Lulu: She wonders if you also heard her fart in class...
Me (I grow stiffer.): What? She did that? Are you joking?? She farted in class? That's weird, isn't it?

P.S. **Lulu looks at me with interrogation marks.

Lulu: What do you mean! Everybody farts once in a while!!
Me: I know, but... Justine?

Lulu: What, Justine? She farts, and... well she does # 2 also, you know, just like the pope, except, if he's like dad, it must smell for a while!!

I burst out laughing!! She makes no sense, but she's hilarious!

She's a leech, but quite a cute one. Even though she GETS ON MY NERVES SOMETIMES, especially when my friends are around. But I kind of like learning SECRETS ABOUT JUSTINE. I absolutely need Lulu in my future FAKE MINISTRY.

Me: Anything else I should know about Justine?

Lulu's face lightens up. **YIPPEEE!!** I'm going to learn so much today!!

{ **We are both startled when mom opens the door **
Her face is tense... }

UH-OH...

Mom (To Lulu): What are you doing here?
Lulu: I thought my big brother could use a snack.
Mom: He can eat later.

I take a quick bite — oh, and another! — before she takes the plate away.

Mom (to Lulu): Out!

Lulu turns to me without saying a thing. I **WINK** at her to **thank her** and she smiles at me before leaving.

My mother glares at me. She's really furious. Common, it's not MY FAULT if Lulu came to my room! I can't be blamed for everything in this house!! I wasn't going to ask her to get out of my room. I'm not rude. I mean, she went out of her way to get me a **snack**!!

**I refrain from commenting. I'm in enough trouble as it is.

Whatever, my mother's never happy about anything. She gets on my nerves, *BIG TIME*, and I think she deserves the **silent treatment** for a few days. Too bad for her. Enough is enough!! I call it bullying (it's true, it's a form of **bullying**. I should give her up to the authorities!).

I'll ignore her for a few days, we'll see how she reacts.

He will last two hours...

Later... = **6:12 pm**

I'd say about *15 MINUTES* before dinner... er... *18 MINUTES*.

There is a knock on my door, but before I can say anything, mom walks in. I look down and try to look busy.

Mom: It's time for dinner. Did you have enough time to think?

> Not looking at her. I pretend to read The Three Musketeers. **SILENT TREATMENT.** I won't break. *I AM STRONGER THAN HER!!*

Mom: Answer me, I am talking to you.

I don't look up, but I shrug. I almost feel like whistling I am in such a defiant mood. (**THERE YOU GO! SILENT TREATMENT!**)

Mom: Well then. I see you still need to think. You can change into your pj's right away. You're going to bed now.

VERY IMPORTANT FACT:

** My stomach **rumbles** and my taste buds are all excited at the idea of a good dinner:

> • I don't know what's cooking, but it smells **really** good.
> • I would say it smells **better** than usual.
> • ARRRGH, she did this on purpose.

He he...

I have NO CHOICE but to answer. The **SILENT TREATMENT** will have to wait until... **dinner**.

That's it! I won't talk to her during dinner. Too bad. But I must give an answer now, because I know her, and she won't change her mind. I won't win. And I'll have to go to bed on an empty stomach...
**WITHOUT EATING DINNER!

The minute she's about to leave, I put the book down and shout (oops.. came out a little higher than expected).

Me (with a shaky voice): Mom, I'm sorry. Please don't be mad.
Mom: I'm not mad. I'm hurt. Nobody likes to be called like that, especially not from their son.
Me: I know. I'm sowwy**.

To myself: «Sowwy?» instead of « I'm sorry »??? AWKWARD. I do that when I get emotional.

Mom: You need to think about the consequences, next time you want to say that to someone.

I **nod** and look down.

VERY IMPORTANT NOTE TO SELF : (EXCEPT FOR MELIA)

Mom: It hurts. And you must understand that you're the only person responsible for your actions. There are consequences.
Me: I understand...

Okay, I get it, so please, enough with the drama!

She leans and gives me a big hug... *OOOOOOH*

I looooove my mom's hugs, they're the best!! Especially when I'm grounded. *OH NO!* Tears are burning my eyes and I'm going to cry.

In my mind, I'm telling myself: Think about something else, Charles!

AH! I KNOW!

MELIA MELIA MELIA MELIA MELIA MELIA
MELIA MELIA MELIA MELIA MELIA MELIA
MELIA MELIA MELIA MELIA MELIA MELIA
MELIA MELIA MELIA MELIA MELIA MELIA
MELIA MELIA MELIA MELIA MELIA MELIA
MELIA MELIA MELIA MELIA MELIA MELIA.

Phew! My emotions have settled down!!

Mom: Common, let's have dinner. It's going to be good!

She leaves. I get emotional again. *GEEZ!* I hate making my mom upset. (What is the matter with me?) I wipe a tear that made its way down my left eye.

Tutu: Are you crying?

**I jump. The little brat was standing in the doorway and saw me. How does he always *appear* like that? He's worse than... you know, that well-known MAGICIAN who does that?

Me: In your dreams. What are you saying?
Tutu: It seemed like you were crying.
Me: Would you stop it with your idiotic questions? Let's go. Time for dinner.

(Taking time to think while going down the stairs.)

I'll never call anyone a b**** ever again... except maybe **Melia**, and **Kevin (he's stupid)**, and, er, that new guy who always wears a red hat. No, he's nice. It's just that, he can be an a** sometimes.

It should be Melia's **official title.** Because she can be really mean to me, sometimes. But I'll keep that... But I'll keep that to myself, so my mom won't know. Although...

May 15th

I took a short break from writing. We have been working hard at school and a lot is going on. I am outside, on the stairs, because the weather is so nice.

First of all: I just saw the best movie *EVER!* And the lead actress is **sooooo** beautiful. I could totally see myself ~~married~~ dating her. He name is... uh... not sure I should write it down. Just in case. Uh. let's call her... hum... Joyce, no, uh, Brenda, no, ~~Justi~~, no... CAT. Okay. Let's call her CAT. Cat looks awesome. Better than Justine. **(Of course, she's a Hollywood actress!)**

William's dad works with people from **Hollywood**. I wonder if he knows someone who knows someone who knows someone who could get me in contact with her. I'm sure we'd get along. She's so beautiful! I want to read the book **(the movie is based on a book, inspired by true events)**. I'll ask mom to get it for me. She won't say no... for a book. Willliam already read it and he **SWEARS** it's excellent.

He actually read it in *TWO DAYS!*

> *P.S.* ** Wow! That's a lot of pages in a short time! But except for eating, William doesn't do much when he's home.

CAT does archery and fencing in the movie. I feel like trying, I'm sure I'd be a natural. And, anyway, I am a musketeer, and the Three Musketeers did archery, right? I'll check it out, I can't remember, even if I just finished (um...) reading it. I sort of skipped a few chapters because it was getting long and boring to read the whole thing.

P.S. **For my book review, I called my cousin Joje and he told me the story in detail. He's soooo cool. The more I think about it, the more I know he'll make a great musketeer.

The Three Musketeers (**Max, William and me**) went to the theater to watch the movie. We went with William's nanny.

**AKA the sheep, because she follows him everywhere.

William's parents are travelling **ONCE AGAIN**. They're never home with their son, and my mother feels sorry for him, that's why he's been coming to our house a lot lately. And we like to walk to the newly opened Dairy Queen near my house. I like Oreo cookie Blizzards. William prefers:

Oreo + Smarties + Brownies + Rolo + caramel topping = too much sugar for me.

He says it's **SICK!** I sure hope so, because it costs

$10 in extras!!!! But his parents give him all the money he wants. I guess they want to make up for never being around.

I fall asleep thinking about **CAT** and what I will tell her when I meet her... *WHAT???* Anything's possible!!! I absolutely have to ask William if his dad knows someone who knows someone who knows someone who could introduce me to her. In the meantime, I'll keep dreaming about her.

Need help?

May 17th

Everywhere in the house, in spite of the nice weather. I'll go outside later.

It's mom's birthday, so dad is organizing a birthday dinner. He's starting the *BBQ*. We haven't *BARBECUED YET* this year, so I'm looking forward to it. Grandma and grandpa are coming over later. *COOL.* I'm sure they'll bring me a present, they always do. I love getting presents, even if the ones they give me are not always fun or cool. (Sometimes, I have to fake a smile and pretend I'm happy about what they offer me. I must be getting good at it because Grandma never catches on.)

Not sure about that.

I go down to the kitchen to see what's going on.

Melia, dad and the twins seem to be working hard. Mom went out for the day to get *PAMPERED* at the **spa**.

That was our birthday + **MOTHER'S DAY** present for her. (The two are almost on the same date this year.)

Me: What are you doing?
Melia: Can't you see? We're building a dog house.

I can see they're making a **cake**.

Me: (I shrug).

I glance at dad who's on the other side of the counter, cutting the beef loin into filets. He loves playing butcher with a huge piece of meat.
(Go figure...)

Melia: You should be helping us instead of watching.
Me: I don't know how to build a dog house.

She wanted to be sarcastic. I know how to play that game.

Lulu: It's easy! You just need to read the instructions!
Melia (To Lulu): He can't read.
Me: HA HA... Very funny, you...

> *P.S.* ** Dad is focused on the steaks.
> I lower my voice.

Me: ...you... big idiot.

Lulu stops breathing. So does Tutu. Melia's eyes pop out of her skull. Lulu's still holding her breath. Until....

Melia: *DAD!!!* Did you hear that?
Dad: No. What?
Melia: Charlie called me an idiot.
Dad (frowning): Hey –
Me: Not true!! She's lying!
Melia: No! **You're** lying!
Dad: I'm warning you both (**Dad has raised the knife, and he's uncomfortable with his bloody hands and the big meat filet– I must bite the insides of my cheeks to keep from laughing), you both better behave tonight at dinner because there will be consequences. Enough is enough! You need to set a good example!
Melia: But he started it!
Dad: I don't care!

> *P.S.* **I smile, Melia crosses her arms.

Dad (very strict tone): You better listen because you'll both be grounded, and for a long time.

P.S. ^{**} **(To myself):** **He actually looks serious. Geez, what's up with that guy? Where's my dad??

Dad: I am talking to you and I am serious. Understood?

[Serious ?? Ha ha. Really?**]**

Me: Yeah yeah.
Dad: No. I don't want to hear "yeah yeah".
Me (confused**):** Uh, you don't actually want to hear "no"??
Dad: Charlie, don't be a smart aleck.
Me: I say "yeah" and that's not okay! What am I supposed to say then?
Dad: I want you to mean it.

P.S. ^{**} I shrug and look up – d-i-s-c-o-u-r-a-g-e-d... I prefer when he doesn't say anything.

Me (and Melia, at the same time): Sorry.

Dad (Okay okay, it's alright... But I want to know you both understand.
Me (I glance at Melia, then): Yes.
Melia (She hesitates, then): Understood.

Melia **pulls a face**... The twins laugh.

I get cookies and pour myself a glass of milk. **I'm too cool. The coolest actually.** Melia is stuck with the twins... and the cake, and I'm going back up to play a video game.

TOTALLY COOL.

CAT would find me charming at this moment.

I'm about to leave the kitchen, snack in hands.

Dad: CHARLIE? What are you doing??
Me (My mouth full of cookies): Eating cookies, why?
Dad: Give us a hand and set up the table.

Dad: Oh! And don't forget grandma and grandpa are coming over, so there'll be eight of us.

Melia gives me a **TRIUMPHANT LOOK**. I deserve it. $1 - 0$ for her. Darn! I must recoup quickly.

<u>Later, when my grandparents arrive:</u>
Around 4:47 PM

I escort my grandma to the living room. Can't wait to see what she got me.

Me: You had a good trip?
Grandma: Ooooh! I loved it! We shopped 'til we dropped, as they say!
Me: Really? Like, what did you buy?
Grandma: Lots of great things!
Grandpa: Tell me about it (he rolls his eyes).

OooooH!! Can't wait to get my present!!

Lulu: What did you get us?
Grandma: Nothing!
Lulu (frowning): Nothing?

I know her, she's joking. What a rascal, my grandma.
I ADOOOORE HER!

Grandma: Really, nothing!

HUH?... SHE CAN'T BE SERIOUS?

Tutu: For real? You're not joking?
Grandma: No. I bought so much stuff for myself I didn't have space left in my luggage.
Grandpa: Tell me about it (he rolls his eyes).

I don't believe it. She's dead serious. She didn't get us
ANYTHING?

Grandma: Not that I didn't want to get you anything, but, you know, you never wear the t-shirts I brought you last time!

Me (To myself): They were so ugly!

P.S. ****** Had I known, I would have worn it on the day she came by.

It's not my best day. NO PRESENTS FROM **MY GRANDPARENTS?!?** This is a first! And grandma keeps repeating she missed me. YEAH RIGHT. She could have brought me a little

something back, to **PROVE SHE REALLY** missed me.
It didn't have to be much. I mean, it's the thought
that counts, right?

Right...

I thought that grandparents were put on this planet
to **spoil** their grandchildren. They have **NOTHING**
else to do... *OH*, except playing cards and golf with
their friends.

I'd rather sleep.

6:59 pm
My nightmare gets even worse at dessert, when the cake is brought to
the table.

EVERYONE: Hap-py birth-day mom-my,
Hap-py birth-day mom-my
Hap-py biiirth-day moooooom-myyyyy!

Happy birthday

TO YOUUU!!

Mom gets emotional.

**Really, she cries for no reason.

Mom: Oh! Thank you!! You are so sweet!!

She looks at the cake from every angle.
(A little annoying)

Mom: It's beautiful!!
Melia: I made it!
Lulu (proud): With me!!
Tutu (proud): And me!!

Mom turns to me, thinking maybe I will say I'm also part of it. I smile at the floor. She looks at the others.

Mom: Thanks guys, you're so sweet.
Me (low voice): I set the table.

No one heard me. At least no one's reacting.

P.S. ** Maybe Melia heard, but she doesn't count.

Mom cuts the cake, and, like I **REALLY** need this...

Grandma (her mouth full): Oh! What a great cake!!
Mom: Mmmm... Yes!!! It's delicious!!
Melia: It's a recipe I found in a magazine.

Blah Blah Blah Blah Blah
Blah Blah Blah Blah

Melia (continuing): I wanted to try something new.
Mom: I hope you kept the recipe, it's great cake.
Lulu, Melia and Tutu: Thanks!

I look around the table... Is everyone ignoring me?

Mom: I must say that –
Me: I set the table.

Everyone turns to me, stunned. I can read on Melia's face:

THAT IS SO IRRELEVANT!!!

P.S. **She's unfortunately right. (2 To 0??)

Mom smiles, and...

Mom: You did?
Me: (I shrug – I don't care... well, a little maybe).

OH NO!

My eyes start burning. I know what this means, but I must keep it together or else Melia will enjoy teasing me about it all year long (and it'll go up to *3549* to *0* for her).

Mom: That's very sweet of you. Thanks, Charlie.

She **WINKS** at me.

Melia: That's why the forks and knives were upside down.

I keep myself from calling her a b***, a c**, an a***, a b****, a... a... At least, the tears are back were they should be.

rong book?

PHEW!!!

Me: That's exactly why, but it's the thought that counts, right?
Mom: Of course, honey!

Melia is furious at me. I finally score a point. *2* To *1*!!

Ha Ha

Harmony back between the kids.

You call this harmony?

June 5th
"**Thinking**" in my room. (**Thinking** = grounded because I put shaving cream in Melia's toothpaste tube... but Lulu used it first.)
BIG MESS.

I haven't written in a while, I'm so busy at school, it's almost illegal. I needed to do a lot of reviewing for exams. I'm a bit stressed out because I don't want to end up having summer school. I'd like to enjoy summer! And my parents said that maybe

** IF MY GRADES ARE GOOD**

I could spend **a week** at a **CAMP**. I've never stayed overnight at camp, because it's always complicated with my parents, but they promised they'd **consider** it if my grades were good. I'd like to go to Max's camp. Actually, I'd prefer going to William's. He spends *SEVEN WEEKS* at a *RICH KIDS'* camp.

***I might miss my family, though, if I left for seven weeks... Err, but not Melia of course.

He tells me it's an amazing place (like a Club Med for teens). I looked it up and there's **NO WAY** my parents could afford it. I don't mind, there are many other places I could go. But first, I need to study hard and get those grades up. *SO, FOCUS CHARLIE!!!*

June 18th

I can't remember what I wanted to write, because today is *JUNE 22ND* but I wanted to mention that the 18th was my last exam. Yesss!!!

I'm done with primary school!

Done with my exams. *OOOPH!* I don't know how I did, but I sure gave it *ALL I HAD*.

Can't wait to get my final **REPORT CARD**. William and Max told me it went great for them and the exams were easy, but we'll see.

When the time comes, like dad would say!!

Max and William are *WAY BETTER* than me at school. But I don't mind. I really put a lot of effort into my studies this year and I think it will pay off.

Mom walks into my room.

Mom: Here's your bag.

I'm going to the country, tomorrow. But not to William's. I'm leaving with the sixth graders for two days to celebrate our **GRADUATION**. I'm very excited to spend a few days with my friends, without my ~~annoying~~ parents! I'm sharing a room with Benjamin, a **FRIEND FROM CLASS**. I would have preferred being with Max or William, but we drew a name, so there was no arguing. It's only one night, anyway. And **Benjamin** is really super nice. I actually wonder why we're not better friends.

Mom: You excited?
Me: Yesssss.
Mom: I'm sure you'll have a lot of fun.

No need to have special powers to figure this one out!
Mom: What are you going to wear to the dance?
Me: Er...

Who cares?

Mom: Are you going to wear a shirt and tie?
Me: A tie?? Are you crazy? My friends will laugh at me!!
Mom: What do you mean! It's a graduation!
Me: Yeah, but not a REAL one!! It's only for sixth grade. I'll keep the tie for high school, thank you very much.

She always goes **overboard**. I mean, really. What sixth grader wears a tie for graduation?

Mom: Alright, but bring it, just in case.
Me: No way!
Mom: Are you at least going to wear a shirt?

Me: Mom?!? Can you just drop it, please? I am NOT wearing a shirt. I'm bringing jeans and a t-shirt.
Mom: No way! You're wearing a nice pair of pants, and it's NON-NEGOTIABLE!
Me: ...

I put the pants in my bag, just so THAT SHE DOESN'T BUG ME (any more). But there's no way I'm wearing them and being laughed at.

Mom: Here's your gel.
Me: Gel?
Mom: For your hair.
Me: Stop it! I'm not going to a wedding!

AAAARGH!! She's so annoying!

Me: Can I be left alone, please?
Mom: Calm down, I just wanted to help and make sure you didn't forget anything.

She kisses me on the forehead before leaving.

I go to bed once I'm done with my bag. I don't know why, but I'm beat, tonight.

June 19th

Although I really try, I can't sleep past *6:11 AM*.

Alone in the kitchen. Oops... Shivers just walked in, not alone anymore! I pour myself a bowl of cereal. Feels awesome to be by myself. **THE WHOLE FAMILY IS STILL ASLEEP. SHIVERS** paws my foot. *OOOOH,* I think someone would like some cereal!

Me: You want some?

I give him some without being reprimanded by my mother.

Me: There you go, big guy.

Shivers wags his tail.

Me: Isn't it great, just the two of us like this? Peace and quiet without the others! I'm going to miss you, you big, hairy dog!

Shivers is staring, and I could swear he understands what I'm saying. I can tell he wants to come with me to the retreat. Can't blame him, really.

Me: Sorry pal, but you can't come. Not that I don't want to bring you, but we're not allo-
Tutu: Are you talking to the dog?!?

I drop my spoon and spill some milk.

Me: Aaaargh!

Tutu startled me. I didn't see him come in.

Me: What are you doing here?
Tutu: Er, I'm allowed in here, it's my kitchen too, you know!
Lulu: Yeah, it's our kitchen, too!

Er, hadn't seen her either.

Me: Keep your kitchen, I'm out!!

Hey, if they think they will intimidate me in my our kitchen, they should think twice. I'd rather be left in peace and quiet in my room anyway. I stand up and leave. Don't feel like putting up with them this morning. I'll be in high school next year, and I'm leaving for my **"GRADUATION PROM"**.

☆ ☆ ☆

We **FINALLY** get to the mountains. *YIPPEEEEE!!* The camp is not as nice as William's ~~castle~~ house, but I'm sure we're going to have fun. We play outside in the woods all afternoon and it's **super nice**. When the bell rings at *4PM,* it's time to get ready for dinner and the dance.

I shower quickly (it's a public shower so I'm not really comfortable, even if we can't see the others) and go back to the room to get dressed. I put my jeans on, as well as a clean t-shirt. Mom made me *PROMISE* to wear something clean, so.... But I didn't promise to wear those fancy pants...

Benjamin walks in the room... er, in a

suit and tie???

Benjamin: Oh, you didn't change yet, Charlie?

ER? Why's he saying that? **"Didn't change"** into what way, exactly?

Me: Er... Is everyone already dressed... like you?

Benjamin: Yesss! We have to be downstairs in 10 minutes!

Me: Okay.

I'm suddenly hot and I don't **FEEL SO GOOD**. I feel like crying / melting into the floor. Am I really **THE ONLY LOSER** without a suit and tie? Oh, and I notice his nice leather shoes and all I have are my Vans sneakers...

I want to die. I'm going to be the laughing stock of the party. I should tell Benjamin to let the others know I don't feel well and I'll just stay in the room the whole night. It feels like I just cut a HUNDRED ONIONS, my eyes are burning so much. How can I get out of this one? I'll be the **class reject** THE ULTIMATE LOSER. **The laughingstock of the evening..** Why did my mom force me to come, I didn't even feel like it...

I feel Benjamin's glance weighing on me like a ton of bricks. If only I had listened to my mo--

I just thought of the perfect excuse! I grab my bag, put it on the bed and search inside.

Me: I thought we were changing after dinner, you know, for the dance! Let me just grab my suit and tie!

Can't believe I'm lying, but it takes what it takes. I'm searching, and searching, and I know that Benjamin's watching me. **(My hands are sweaty)**.

Me: Oooooooh nooooooooooooooooooooooo!?!?!?!?!?
Benjamin: What's wrong?
Me: My mom forgot to pack my suit and tie!
Benjamin: Your mom? You can't pack your own bag for yourself at your age?

ER...

Me: She... forced me to let her do it because she wanted to do it herself!!
Benjamin: Forced??
Me: Er...

Should I have used the word: **BOUND?**
COMPELLED?

Benjamin: Yikes, and I thought Max was only kidding when he said your mom was as tough as an Army general.
Me: Er... He said that?

She's not **THAT** bad. I pull out the fancy pants she **DID** force me to bring.

(PHEW)

Me: I only have this pair of pants.

Benjamin thinks for a moment. He opens his bag, pulls out a blue tie, takes his orange tie off and hands it to me.

Me: What are you doing?
Benjamin: Put the orange one on. It'll look cooler with your t-shirt.
Me: What about you?
Benjamin: I'll wear the blue one.
Me: Yeah, but you had put the orange one on.
Benjamin: Who cares! Common, hurry up!
Me: I look stupid with my sneakers on.
Benjamin: No! They're super cool! Oh I have an idea!!

He takes his **nice shoes off**. Is he really going to lend them to me? He has really tall feet. He takes his pair of sneakers.

Me: You wearing that?
Benjamin: Yup.
Me: You can't do that! It looked... neater with the other ones.
Benjamin: Yeah, but it's much cooler with the Converse. And there'll be two of us. Less embarrassing, don't you think?

OMG!! What a cool guy!! Why's he doing that for me??

Benjamin: Because you've always been cool to me, Charlie. And you came to my defense in fourth grade when I got bullied by Kevin. I've always been too embarrassed to thank you, because I was ashamed.

OOPH... I feel like something is stuck in my throat. *EMOTIONS, MAYBE?* I remember exactly what happened, but I didn't realize it was bullying back then.

Benjamin: And, between you and me, sneakers are so much more comfortable!!
He winks at me. I smile, letting go of all my emotions.

PHEW!

Max and William walk in... both in suit and tie!!

William: What are you doing?
Me: Er... We were just getting ready to go.
Benjamin: Look how cool Charlie is! I switched my shoes to be like him! It'll be more comfortable to dance in sneakers!!
Max: That's so true!!!
William: Yeah! Hey, Charlie, do you mind if I change my shoes, too? These are so uncomfortable!
Max: Yeah! Mind if I do, too?

WHAT!? They really want to be like me?!?

Cooooooooool!!!!

** I always knew I was a cool guy.

Uh, hum.

Me: Sure!!! We'll wait for you!! But I don't have a jacket...

William: Who cares? I kind of like the t-shirt with the tie! I would copy you if could!!

He can't be serious?!

Max: I agree! Pretty cool look, Charlie!!

William: We'll be right back!

They leave. Benjamin raises an eyebrow. He's very happy he can "repay" me with a favour. Our eyes lock for many seconds.

Me: Thank you.

Benjamin: No, Charlie, Thank YOU.

Great guy, Benjamin. **Too bad** we won't be at the same school next year...

The evening's going well and everyone's complimenting my outfit! It's *SOOOOOO COOL!* I'm the only one **without a jacket**, but all my friends are sort of jealous of me! Even Oliver, our future designer in the gang told me I was avant-garde!!

We all go crazy on the dance floor, and at the end of the night, the **DJ** plays a slow song. Justine is staring at me from the other side of the room.
Er... What does she want from me?

William: Ask her to dance.
Me: Are you crazy!

William: Why not? I know you like her! Look around, a lot of guys are dancing with girls. No big deal.
Me: Not me. I'm staying with you.
William: You're an idiot.

ER...

Me: Excuse me?
William: You heard me. No one wants to dance with me because I'm fat, but I would've liked to. You have a chance and you don't want to. Dancing with her doesn't commit you for life, you know?
Me: I know, but...
William: But what? She's been staring at you for the past hour almost!!
Me: We're kind of far apart, maybe it's you she's staring at...

I turn my back at her not to see her anymore. **It's too embarrassing**.

William: You're all excuses, Charlie. Look, you know I'm always on your side, right? But if you don't ask her, you're going to regret it in the morning.

HMM... What if he's right? No time for an answer, Max is here.

Max: What are you doing?

ER...

William: He was actually on his way over there, right Charlie?

He knocks me kindly in the belly... *COMMON.*

AAARGH... I'm too shy. William glances above my shoulder at the same time I feel a hand on my shoulder. I turn around.

Me: Justine?
Justine: Want to dance?

ER... ER... ER... ER...

Me: O...kay.

We get to the dance floor and I grab her waist. OH! It's smaller than it looks... We stay silent during the XX MINUTES of the song, but I think... Is it possible this version is shorter than the one playing on the radio? Because it feels like we only danced for a few seconds. SHAME! I was kind of enjoying it...

I go to bed happy. I danced a "slow" with Justine. Life's kind of cool, isn't it?

June 22nd
In class – we're all done for the year.

LAST DAY OF SCHOOL. It's raining outside. We brought board games and we're all playing in different groups. What's cool is that we were allowed to bring food.

very important...

But we must be careful, because there are <u>FIVE PEOPLE</u> with allergies in our class:

- Veronica (the magpie)
- Kevin (not the idiot, another one)
- William (not the fat one, another one)
- François-Xavier, the hyper active guy (Sometimes I really feel like giving him a nut to calm him down)
- That new guy with the red baseball cap. I always forget his name. ✱

✱ It's about time I got his name right, it's the end of the year. (And he's not really new anymore, because he's been at my school for five years. **TO MY DEFENSE**, his name is very... exotic. It's something like Jarof, Yabof, Yamorv, I don't know. No one ever remembers, not even **MISS HOWARD. She always gets it wrong.** Who cares, I'll remember next year...

William's mom bought (because she never cooks) cupcakes for the whole class!!

It was nice of her. But I think she should spend the effort taking care of her son. **My mom says it's none of our business. And we should mind our own business.**

Right before the bell rang, we all said:

BYE BYE!

Have a great summer, and see you next year!!

> ** Technically, it's wrong to say that, because we'll be seeing each other this year, but at the end of the summer. I don't get it.

Haven't received my report card yet. I don't know how my summer's going to shape up, except for that soccer day camp.

Knowing my mom, she has probably bought **EXERCISE BOOKS FOR MATHS AND ENGLISH** so I can practice. I'll do them when I'm grounded... Or I'll write in this ~~diary~~ notebook (**or a new one, because there are only a few pages left in this one**) and describe my summer.

I'll see my friends for sure. **Especially Max**. William's going away to that rich kids' camp for **SEVEN WEEKS**. (Er... Have I mentioned that already? Haven't had time to re-read what I've written down in this book.) Anyway, I won't be seeing a lot of him this summer. That **SUCKS, BIG TIME**.

I'll play tennis at the park, and oh, I'll catch a few frogs for Melia.

HA HA

**But my mom CAN'T ever find out, though, which is almost...

IMPOSSIBLE

Right before leaving, I go to my locker, and then to the fountain to drink some water. As I get up from the fountain, I notice Justine standing right next to me.

Me: Oh, hi!
Justine: Here.

She hands me a piece of paper. I frown: "What is this??

She sort of read my mind because she answers before I ask the question.

Justine: My email address, if you feel like writing me this summer.

Justine is not on social media.

Me: Cool.
Justine: What are you doing this summer?
Me: Don't know much yet.

Me: You?
Justine: Going to my grandma's for a week and then camp for two more.
Me: Cool...
Justine: Okay, well, bye then...

She leans and kisses me VERY QUICKLY ON THE LIPS. Actually, it wasn't really on the lips, because I sort of turned around on the same side she did, so our lips touched lightly.

WHAT EVER.

Never washing my mouth ever again. **NO JOKE** (or almost).

I wish Willow kissed me at the dog run.

A few days later...

I don't know at what time the discussion started because I didn't pay attention, but it ended at *10:52 AM*.

Mom walks into my room.

Mom: Charlie?
Me: What?
Mom: I have good news.

*** **GOOD NEWS?** Hmm, I'm holding my breath, because we never know what **good news** means with my mom: "You won a trip around the corner with the dog." See what I mean?

Mom: Dad and I have decided to send you to camp for two weeks.
Charlie: Oh... yeah?

I know I don't sound excited, but my parents aren't the coolest in the world. They're probably sending me to this LOOOOSER camp and think I should be excited.

GEEZ! Once again, I'm going to have to fake that I'm happy. (I'm getting good at it, though...)

Mom: I spoke to Jess, Max's mom, and you'll be going at the same time.
Me: ... er... same time... same camp?
Mom: Of course!! We wouldn't have sent you just anywhere! And I also spoke to Stef, and your cousin Joje will also be going!
Me (my eyes get bigger.): At the same time?

Mom nods.

I jump on her!!

Me: Thank youuuuuuuuu!!! You guys are so cooooooool!!!!!

P.S. ** It's written bigger because I'm so happy.

P.S. ** If this notebook was bigger, I would have written bigger!

Anyone has the right to change his mind. My mom can be cool... er, sometimes... rarely but... er, sometimes.

I call Max quickly.

Me: Guess what??
Max: What?
Me: We're going to camp together!!!!
Max: Yesssssss!!!

Me: And my cousin Joje. You're finally going to meet him!

Max: Awesome!!

We'll have *PLENTY OF TIME* to find a name for our country and write a **LEGAL CONSTITUTION**. William won't be there, but we can send him emails.

SEE YOU SOON!!!

This publication was printed on recycled paper on January 30th, Two Thousand and Twenty Four,
for Forbidden Press Books inc.